"So where's your *kind of* boyfriend tonight?" Scott asked.

The lazy way he said it—and the way his arm seemed to accidentally brush along the length of mine as he leaned back—made my heart do a little cartwheel.

"Milwaukee," I said, my voice breaking a little.

Now his leg was right beside mine, his hip against mine, the whole length of our bodies just barely touching as we sat facing forward, not looking at each other.

"How come you didn't go?"

I shrugged, not knowing what else to do.

"Well, good thing you stayed home." He tossed his cigarette butt down and stubbed it out with his foot.

"Why?"

"Because . . ." Scott said. He turned to me, took the half-smoked cigarette out of my hand, and stubbed it out too.

For a moment we just stared at each other through the twilight, his eyes searching mine. I couldn't turn away or speak or even breathe.

Then Scott leaned over and kissed me.

2

TURNING
seventeen

More Than This

by Wendy Corsi Staub

A PARACHUTE PRESS BOOK

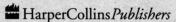 HarperCollins*Publishers*

Created and produced by
PARACHUTE PUBLISHING, L.L.C.
156 Fifth Avenue, Suite 302
New York, NY 10010

Published by
HarperCollins*Publishers*
1350 Avenue of the Americas
New York, NY 10019

First HarperCollins*Publishers* printing, August 2000

HarperCollins® and ▄▄®
are trademarks of HarperCollins*Publishers*, Inc.

Library of Congress Catalog Card Number: 00-100947
ISBN 0-06-447238-8

Printed in the U.S.A.

10 9 8 7 6 5 4 3 2 1

Design by AFF Design
Cover photos by Anna Palma
Hair and makeup by Julie Matos for Oribe Salon

More Than This

Chapter 1

"**G**od, I'm late," I whispered as I rushed up the three steps to my boyfriend Alex McKay's house. It was Friday, and we were supposed take his four-year-old nephew, Josh, to get some pizza on the way to the South Central High football game. But there was no way we'd make it now.

I knocked a few times on the front door, then opened it. "Hey, it's me," I called, stepping into the foyer.

"In here, Jess," Alex yelled from the kitchen.

I found him at the sink, washing a pot. He looked so cute standing there in his khakis and denim shirt. His short, wavy brown hair had a few soapsuds in it. "Sorry I'm late," I said.

"No problem," Alex replied. "I called Erin and Maya and told them to save seats for us." Erin Yamada and Maya Greer were two of my best friends. "How did your research go?" he asked.

I leaned on the counter and sighed. "So, I spent all afternoon at the university library, trying to do research for that Emily Dickinson paper, right? And I found, like, one book. That college library is just too huge. I wish I could just do my research at South Central. It would make my life a lot easier."

Alex placed the pot in the sink, and gave me a tiny kiss on my nose. He took my hands. "Yeah, but you were never about making your life easy. That's why you're taking college classes in the first place, right?"

He pulled me into a warm hug, and I rested my head on his chest. "I guess so."

I was the only senior at our high school taking courses at the University of Wisconsin. I had tested into a special program that allowed me to combine my senior year of high school with my freshman year of college. A big honor. But I never realized that college would be so hard. I mean, school had always come easy for me, but now, in college, I actually had to work for my grades.

"And I guess Emily Dickinson's poetry is cool," I added, still holding Alex. "But she sounds a little psycho." I glanced up at his handsome face. "Did you know she never left her house? How weird is that?"

"Aunt Jessie, you're here!" Josh cried as he bounded into the room.

I smiled to myself. Josh had just started calling

me Aunt Jessie. I thought it was really cute.

"I'm here!" I answered, breaking from Alex, and swinging Josh around. "Are you starving?"

"Yeah, but Uncle Alex said we can get pizza at the confession stand 'cause there's no time to stop now."

"Concession stand," Alex corrected with a grin.

"Well, then let's get your coat on," I told Josh.

"I can do it," Josh insisted. He ran to the coat rack near the back door and grabbed his jacket. He struggled to put it on by himself, so I walked over to help.

"Are you finished washing that pot?" I asked Alex.

"Just about. My folks were late for their bowling league, and Mom left it to soak. I figured I'd do it while I was waiting for you."

He's amazing, I thought. Most guys would just leave it in the sink, but not Alex. Busy as he was with school stuff, he tried to help out around the house, and with Josh.

Both of Alex's parents worked full-time. His older brother David was Josh's father. David and his wife, Betsy, shared a bedroom with Josh in the small house. They both worked part-time and went to college. And I thought they were pretty lucky to have Alex around to help them with their son.

We headed out the door with Josh between us, holding our hands and swinging our arms.

"Daddy!" Josh yelled, as an old blue Chevy pulled up to the curb.

David got out, wearing his black-and-white waiter's uniform. He looked beat. "Hey, Bub," he said to Josh. He always called him that, and every time he did, Josh got this big grin on his face.

"Daddy, we're going to a football game."

"Wow, that's great," David said. He glanced at Alex and me. "Thanks for taking him."

"No problem," Alex replied.

I felt sorry for David as the three of us headed to Alex's mom's car. I mean, there he was watching his son go off holding hands with somebody else. But what else could he do? He got Betsy pregnant when they were both sixteen. Between work and school, they didn't have much free time to spend with their son. I glanced at Josh. I guess I kind of felt sorry for him too.

When Alex and I have a family, it'll be so different, I thought. We'll be older, settled in our careers, and we'll have a place of our own. We'll be really happy together, just like we are now.

"Can I have pepperoni on my pizza?" Josh asked as I strapped him into his car seat.

"Definitely. Extra cheese too." I gave him a big fat kiss on the cheek. Josh squirmed and giggled.

"That's what I love about you, Jess," Alex said

4

when I got into the front seat.

My heart skipped a beat. "What do you love about me?" I asked, trying to sound casual, but dying to know.

"You're so kind to people—especially to Josh. You go out of your way to be nice to everyone. You would never hurt anyone."

"Not if I could help it," I told Alex. "But you wouldn't, either. That's what I love about you."

Actually, there were a lot of things I loved about Alex. The way I could always count on him. The fact that he always let me know he loved me. . . . But there was one thing that really bothered me.

Sex.

Not that he ever pressured me, like people might expect. The problem was just the opposite. We'd been going out since sophomore year and we'd barely gone past making out. I was starting to wonder if it was as hard for Alex to put on the brakes as it was for me. He always seemed so in control, so able to do the right thing.

I knew he thought the right thing was to wait because he didn't want us to end up like David and Betsy. But we could take precautions, couldn't we? We could be safe. We didn't have to wait till we were married . . . did we?

Sometimes I wondered if that was what Alex had

in mind. I couldn't come right out and ask him because, well, we just didn't talk about that kind of stuff.

Maybe we should, I thought. *Maybe I should get up my nerve one of these days, and bring it up.*

"Jessie, I have to go to the bathroom," Josh said, tugging my sleeve.

I tore my gaze away from my younger brother, Ricky, who had just made a tackle out on the football field. Everyone stood and cheered as they stomped their feet on the green wooden bleachers. Ricky spiked the ball onto the grass, and did a little victory dance. From somewhere above me in the crowded stands, I could hear my parents yelling his name at the top of their lungs. How embarrassing.

"I'll take you, Josh," Alex offered. He sat on Josh's other side and glanced at me over the boy's head.

"I want to go to the ladies' room with Aunt Jessie."

"But you're a boy. Boys go to the men's room," Alex said firmly. He took him by the hand, leading him along the bleachers.

"Oh, my God, he's so sweet, Jessica," Erin said.

"I know. Isn't he adorable?" I watched Alex help Josh climb down to the row below.

"Who?" Maya asked. "Alex or Josh?" She was sitting on the other side of Erin.

"Both, actually," I told her with a grin.

"Oh, great, there's my dad over there shaking everyone's hands," she said, rolling her eyes.

I looked down a few rows and saw Mr. Greer. He was a high-profile lawyer with the DA's office. It wasn't official yet, but Maya said he'd probably run for lieutenant governor of Wisconsin in the upcoming election.

"I can't believe he wore a suit and tie to a football game," Maya complained. "Lately it's as if he's always campaigning, every minute of his life. I think he's trying to get a head start on the election. I bet that's the only reason he's here."

We watched the last play of the quarter and stood up to clap. Then the team jogged off the field and into the locker room. The cheerleaders lined up on the orange track that circled the field, and cried out a victory cheer. Then they took a break.

Our friend Kerri Hopkins put down her navy-and-gold pompoms, and gazed up into the bleachers, looking for us.

"Up here, Ker!" Erin stood on the bench and waved. She was Japanese-American and had the most gorgeous black hair. Lately she'd been wearing it with streaks of purple for dramatic effect. It fanned around her face as she tried to get Kerri's attention.

Kerri grinned and made her way up, pulling her

wool cheerleader's jacket on over her short uniform. Her long blond hair was tousled from cheering and jumping around. But somehow, while anyone else would have looked awful, messed-up hair looked great on Kerri. I thought her bare legs must freeze during these games, but she never seemed to mind.

"What's up, guys?" she asked, plopping down on the bench in front of us. "Did you see Ricky's tackle, Jessica?"

"Yeah, he's playing great tonight," I replied. "My mom will probably come home with laryngitis."

"Hi, Maya," a voice said.

I turned and saw Luke Perez in the row behind us. He was really cute, but I had never heard him say much. He always seemed kind of shy. Now he was giving Maya this look—one that said he was really into her.

It wasn't surprising. Maya looks just like her Argentinean mom, who passed away about two years ago. Big, brown, exotic eyes, longish dark hair, olive complexion.

"Oh, hey, Luke," Maya said, then turned back to us as if she could care less that a cute boy wanted to talk to her.

She's very quiet around guys, and doesn't date much—actually not at all. Except for that one time she met up with T.J. Miller, that jerk from the basketball team. She was totally crushing on him, and he forced himself on her. Thank God she got away before he really hurt her. But still, Maya was probably a little messed up over that—I know I would be. And I didn't see her trusting another guy anytime soon.

Erin nudged her. "Talk to him, Maya. He's still staring at you," she said under her breath. "He's got 'You're hot' written all over his face."

Maya ignored Erin and started talking to Kerri. "So have you gotten any more e-mails from your dad?"

Kerri stiffened. "You mean from the loser?" she asked. It was obvious she didn't want to talk about her father—especially since she'd found out that he'd been living in Milwaukee for years. He'd never once come to see her in Madison. "All I have to say on that subject is . . . delete. Didn't even read them."

Erin glanced at me. I knew what she was thinking. *Kerri sounds as if she doesn't care about her dad anymore, but I'm not buying it.*

I didn't buy it either.

"Listen, I just heard about this party tonight at Amy Presser's house," Kerri said, changing the subject. "Her parents are in Bermuda. You guys want to go?"

"I'd love to, but I should stick with Alex," I told her. "He has to get Josh home to bed. And then he has to get up super early tomorrow for that yearbook seminar in Milwaukee, so he probably won't want to go anyway."

"Aren't you going with him?" Erin asked.

"Can't. I have a huge test on Monday in sociology, and there's this paper on Emily Dickinson due soon. And my writing group is meeting next week, and I have nothing to show them. I don't know how I'm going to get it all done in time."

"That's what you always say," Erin chimed in. "But you always manage to be superstudent anyway. Hey, maybe I should make you a cape for Christmas!"

"Ha, ha," I said. She had no idea how hard it was to juggle everything. And I really wanted to go to Milwaukee with Alex. It would have been a cool thing to do together. Besides, I deserved to go. I'd worked hard on the yearbook for the last three years in order to be features editor.

"Well, I'm definitely going to Amy's," Erin said.

"Not me," Maya added.

"Because of your dad?" I asked her. Maya's father was even stricter than mine.

"I just don't feel like it, okay?" Maya said in a tone that made it obvious that she didn't want to talk about it. Before any of us could say a word, Alex came back with Josh, who was holding a hot pretzel dripping with yellow mustard.

"Hey, Alex, do you mind if Jess goes to a party with us after the game?" Erin asked him.

"I told you. I can't go. I've really got to study," I insisted.

"Come on, Jess. You have all weekend to study," Erin argued.

"Not really. I have to go to a stupid barbecue at the Seiferts' with my parents on Saturday. And then I have that student council thing at Amber Brawley's house on Sunday. Don't forget, you guys said you'd come over to help make posters for the fund-raiser."

"Wait a sec," Kerri said. "Let's go back to the important part—you're going to the *Seiferts'*?"

I nodded. Mr. and Mrs. Seifert were good friends with my parents. "I tried to get out of it, but my parents aren't having it."

"Did you hear Scott Seifert is back home?" Kerri went on. "He was going to Columbia in New York City, and then his father lost his job and he had to transfer back to the university here this semester. Haven't you run into him on campus?"

"Scott Seifert?" I asked, only half paying attention. I knew all about the Seiferts' money problems, and I didn't find them half as fascinating as Kerri seemed to. "No. Why?"

"Because I saw him at Starbucks, and he's totally hot," Kerri replied.

"Really?" I wasn't surprised. I hadn't seen Scott lately, but he was always cute in a scruffy way. Not my type, though. My type, basically, was Alex, I thought, glancing at him. He was wiping mustard off Josh's face, not really paying attention to our conversation.

"Find out if Scott has a girlfriend, okay?" Kerri told me.

I narrowed my eyes. "A, I bet he won't even be there, and B, who cares if he has a girlfriend or not? You have a boyfriend, remember? Matt? That cute football player you're crazy about?"

"Give me a break, Jess. I'm just curious. I wouldn't cheat on Matt any more than you'd cheat on Alex," Kerri said, glancing over her shoulder. "Hey, the players are back. I'd better get down there. See you guys later."

"What was that about you cheating on me?" Alex asked, crumpling the mustard-stained napkin and shoving it into the pocket of his jacket.

"Didn't you hear? There's another man in Jessica's life," Erin said.

I grinned. "Yeah, Alex, you'd better look out."

"Oh, no," he said, pretending to be all upset. "I knew I couldn't hang on to you forever. Who is he?"

"His name is Josh, and I'm crazy about him," I said, reaching past Alex to tickle his nephew.

Josh squealed with laughter, and we all cracked up.

"I'm really glad I skipped Amy's party," I told Alex as we cuddled on the couch in his living room later that night. I draped my legs across his lap, and kissed him sweetly on the lips. It felt so good being in his arms. So comfortable.

Alex pulled me closer and kissed me back. "Me too," he whispered. Delicious sensations ran through my body as he kissed my neck and ran his hands through my hair and under my shirt. I closed my eyes, not wanting him to stop.

But he did. He took my hand and started playing with my fingers. "I guess I'd better drive you home," he said.

"We can hang out a little longer." I leaned closer, and nuzzled his neck. "It's so cozy on the couch like this. I'm not in a hurry."

Alex kissed the top of my head. I turned and tilted my face upward, and he kissed my mouth. A longer, deeper kiss.

My heart started pounding like crazy. I wanted to be closer to him. As close as I could possibly be.

He lifted his lips, and softly brushed his mouth against my ear. "I've got to get you home. Your curfew . . ."

"Don't worry," I told him. "My parents went to my aunt and uncle's for coffee after the game. They'll definitely stay there a while, bragging about Ricky." I leaned in for another kiss.

"That's not exactly what I'm worried about." Alex cleared his throat. "I've got to get up early, and . . ." His voice trailed off.

I figured he wanted me to say something, but I felt really weird all of a sudden. I mean, wasn't he supposed to be the one who wanted things to go further? Wasn't I supposed to be the one backing off, and saying I should get home? Wasn't he as crazy about me as I was about him?

Obviously not.

"Why are you looking at me like that?" he asked.

"Like what?"

"Like you're really upset all of a sudden."

"Because I am," I said, pulling back from him. I had to bring up our sex life—or the fact that we didn't have one. I swallowed hard and took a deep breath.

It's now or never, I decided. I just hoped that what I was about to say would only change things between us for the better.

Chapter 2

■ gazed into Alex's warm brown eyes for a moment, trying to find the right words. "It's just . . . well, whenever we're alone together and things get, you know . . . it's like you're not really that into it. You're always pulling away from me. I mean, it makes me feel kind of . . . stupid, you know? Like you don't want . . ." I stopped, suddenly feeling like an idiot. Alex was staring at me as if I was a complete nutcase.

"You don't think I want you?" he asked. "Oh, my God, Jessica, I *so* want you. Totally. Absolutely." He shook his head like he couldn't believe what I had just said. "Can't you tell?"

"I guess not," was the lame answer I came up with. Now I really felt like a jerk. I wished I'd never started this whole thing, but it was too late to take it back now.

He reached out and brushed my cheek with the

back of his hand. "Don't you think I want us to be together?"

"It doesn't seem as if you do. I mean, we haven't even come close."

"Not because I don't want to," Alex replied. "I think about it every time we're alone together. But look at David. Look at his life. He used to be this fun guy, with tons of friends, talking about going away to college, playing sports. Now he's got a wife and a kid, and he can't even support them on his own. He works at a diner, and takes a few courses when he can squeeze them in. Who knows when he'll ever finish college, or get a real job? He never sees Betsy, and when he does, they have nothing to say to each other anymore. It's as if they don't even *like* each other. I don't want that to happen to us, Jess."

"I don't either," I said. "It doesn't have to."

"Not if we don't let it," Alex cut in. "And there's only one way to make sure. By not taking any chances."

"But we could be careful, Alex," I began. "Or we can be together in other ways." I felt dumb arguing with him about it, but couldn't he see that there might be some solution here? "I just want us to get closer."

"I know," Alex replied. "I do too. Believe me. But the further we go, the harder it is for me to stop. It's too risky. With you, I won't be able to stop."

I knew what he'd said about David and Betsy was

true, but somehow it sounded like an excuse. Maybe deep down, he really didn't find me as irresistible as he claimed to.

Alex sat there, stroking my hand, with this totally understanding look on his face. *Should I keep arguing with him?* I wondered. *No. What's the point?* I turned away.

"I didn't mean to hurt your feelings, Jess," he said gently, still touching my hand. "Some guys might just say, 'Sure. Okay, let's do it.' But I know what can happen, and I'm trying to look out for you too."

"I understand," I said. And I did. Mostly. At this stage in our lives, sex—whether you ended up having it or not—was a big deal no matter how you looked at it. And Alex wasn't some insensitive jerk. I knew I was lucky that way. I just didn't feel particularly lucky at that exact moment.

"Listen, I should really take you home," he said. "It's late, and—"

"I know, you've got to get up early. Have a good time tomorrow. I wish I could bc there with you."

"Yeah, well, I know you've got to study."

"And go to that stupid barbecue with my parents," I added.

We both stood up and walked to the hall closet. He opened the door, reached in and handed me my jacket. "Maybe it won't be so bad."

"Trust me, it will," I said, buttoning up. "Meanwhile, you'll be in Milwaukee having a great time."

He grabbed his keys, and we walked to the door. "Let's get together when I get home. I should be back around seven. What time is the barbecue over?"

"Who knows? I'll call you from the Seiferts'. Maybe my parents can drop me off here on the way home," I said, as I slid into his car.

"That would be great. And listen, don't forget to write down your ideas for yearbook features. I need them Monday morning."

"They're due Monday?" I groaned. "One more thing to worry about this weekend. Great."

He got this pretend-stern look on his face. "As your editor-in-chief, I hope I can count on you to pull your weight on the staff, Ms. Carvelli."

"At your service, Mr. McKay." I saluted.

Then I turned to open the door, hoping he didn't see the disappointed look on my face.

I unlocked the front door to our two-story colonial house in Kensington Heights, and waved back at Alex, who was standing by the curb. When he saw I was inside, he got back into his mom's car and started the engine.

"Jessica? Is that you?" my mother called.

"Yeah." I shut the door behind me and took a deep breath. It was half an hour past my curfew.

"You're late," my father said when I walked into the kitchen. He and my mother were sitting at the table with a pile of bills, a checkbook, and a calculator. Dad was still wearing the South Central High sweatshirt and jeans he'd worn to the game, but my mother had on her flannel nightgown and a terrycloth robe that had seen better days.

I kissed both of them on the cheek. "Sorry. Hey, I thought you were going over to Aunt Deb and Uncle Richie's house," I said, opening the fridge and taking out a can of soda.

"We did, but we didn't stay long," my mother said. "Uncle Richie has to work the early shift tomorrow. What did you think of your brother's game?"

"Great," I said.

"I saw a couple of college scouts in the crowd," Dad said. "They seemed to take a real interest in Ricky. An athletic scholarship to college would be a huge help," he added, a comment he made after every game.

My mother glanced at the pile of bills. "Three of you in college—how are we going to manage?"

My sister, Lisa, was in her sophomore year at Marquette. It was expensive, and my mother—who had never worked outside the house in her life—had recently taken a job as a part-time secretary.

My parents wanted me to continue my studies at the University of Wisconsin next year. The school had a good English department, and I really liked taking courses there, but I had no intention of staying at home after this year. I wanted to go someplace exciting, where I could experience life without my parents looking over my shoulder all the time. A place where I didn't have to be perfect Jessica Carvelli—where I could write, and make mistakes, and just be free.

I had already brought up the subject of New York University in Manhattan a couple of times. My parents knew I wanted to apply there, and to a bunch of other schools. They were far from enthusiastic. I figured now wasn't a good time to bring it up again. Not with all these bills spread out all over the place.

That was another reason I had to get great grades in my college courses this term. If I bombed out, my parents would have another excuse to make me stay home next fall. And they definitely didn't need any more ammunition.

"Well, I guess I'll go to bed," I said.

"Don't forget we have that barbecue at the Seiferts' tomorrow," my mother called after me as I headed for the stairs.

"Do I really have to go? I have a ton of studying to do."

"You're going," my parents replied in unison.

"Besides, you can study on Sunday," my mother said. "After we come back from Grandma's."

Every Sunday afternoon, the entire family converged at my grandmother's house for lunch right after church. It was a total mob scene, but at least my grandmother was a great cook.

"I don't have time on Sunday either. I have to go to a student council meeting—we have to get ready for a fund-raiser that's happening on Monday."

"Well, you'll just have to figure it out," my father said in his end-of-discussion tone. He put on his reading glasses and picked up the stack of bills. "But you're coming to the barbecue. You and Ricky both."

"Fine. Then I'll have to get up really early tomorrow to get my work done. Like, at the crack of dawn—"

"Go to bed, Jessica." My father cut me off. "I don't want to hear it right now. Your mother and I have a lot on our minds."

"So do I," I shot back, and stomped up the stairs to my room.

I did have a lot on my mind. My life was definitely getting intense. And I couldn't believe my parents were going to drag me along to that stupid barbecue tomorrow. *Maybe I'll pull an Emily Dickinson*, I thought, *and refuse to leave the house.*

Yeah, right. My parents would really love that.

Chapter 3

"This is totally unfair," I muttered in the car on the way over to the Seiferts'. I was really annoyed that my brother had gotten out of it, saying he'd hurt himself in last night's game and needed to keep his leg elevated.

"Jessica." My mother twisted around to look at me in the backseat. "Don't start."

My father didn't say anything, just turned up the Barry Manilow song on the easy listening station.

I glanced out the window at the boring suburban houses of Kensington Heights—all two-story colonials like our own. All painted white, with black shutters. I was really starting to hate this place. I couldn't wait until I was away at college, and then I could finally spend my weekends my way.

I debated arguing some more with my mother, but decided it wasn't worth it. Instead I changed my tactic. "It just doesn't sound like much fun. Who am

I supposed to hang around with at the Seiferts'?"

"You can hang around with us," my father said.

My mother laughed. "Ted and Rosie will be so glad you came, Jessica. The girls will too—you know how they look up to you."

The girls were Scott Seifert's eight-year-old twin sisters, who were always following me around. I had to admit, the hero worship was kind of flattering. On the other hand, they were only eight, so what did they know?

"I wonder if Scott will be around." My mother pulled down her visor mirror to check her lipstick.

At the mention of his name, my father shook his head and clucked his tongue. He said, as he always did, "Poor Ted and Rosie. What they did to deserve that kid, I'll never know."

My mother nodded in agreement.

I rolled my eyes. I mean, jeez, it wasn't as if Scott was a serial killer or anything. He was just a little different—kind of a loner. But around Kensington Heights, that was practically a crime.

We pulled up in front of the Seiferts' two-story colonial. It looked a lot like ours, and so did their development.

My mother made me help her take a bunch of covered glass Corningware dishes out of the trunk while my father looked through the glove compartment for a cassette tape he wanted to give to Mr. Seifert.

I hoped the Seiferts wouldn't be offended by all the food my mother had brought. It looked as though she thought they were starving or something, with Mr. Seifert out of work.

"They're here, Mom!" one of the twins, probably Megan, shouted from inside. The front door was open. It was one of those Indian summer days that always made you forget that school had started again. I wasn't even wearing a jacket, just a short-sleeved T-shirt tucked into a pair of old jeans.

The screen door was flung open, and Megan came bouncing out across the lawn. "Hi, Jessica. Hi, Mrs. Carvelli. Hi, Mr. Carvelli. Wow, are these brownies?" She lifted a corner of the foil on the dish my mom was holding. "Scott loves brownies."

"Look who's here." Rose Seifert stuck her head out the front door. "Jessica, I'm so glad you came. The girls have been asking me all day if you'd be here." She was such a nice woman, short and chubby, with flushed cheeks and curly dark hair.

Ted Seifert came around through the side yard, wearing a "Kiss the Chef" barbecue apron and carrying a pair of giant tongs. He greeted everyone in his loud, booming voice, kidding my father about donning an apron and taking over at the grill. It was

24

hard to believe he had a care in the world.

As soon as I put the food down in the kitchen, Megan pulled me toward the stairs. Her twin, Maura, shyly tagged along, and we all headed toward their bedroom.

Music blared from the first room at the top of the stairs. That, I remembered, was Scott's room. The door was halfway open. Across the hall, the bathroom door was closed. I could hear the shower running.

"Scott's in there," Maura said. "He just got up."

"Now?" I glanced at my watch. It was past three o'clock.

"He got home really late last night," Megan said, then pulled me into their room. "Come on. Let's play a game."

"What do you want to play?" I asked, already a little bored. I wasn't really in the mood for this.

"Hey," I heard someone say.

I spun around in the direction of the voice. Scott stood in the doorway with one hand propped against the frame. He had obviously just come out of the bathroom.

He looked . . . okay, I hated to say Kerri was right, but he looked totally amazing!

His dark hair, wet from his shower, was shorter than it had been the last time I saw him, but it was still wavy and just grazing his shoulders. His black eyes were narrowed in his usual brooding stare.

But the major thing about him, the thing that was impossible to ignore, was that he wasn't wearing a shirt—just a pair of faded jeans, and a towel draped around his neck.

I couldn't find my voice to even say hello. I kept glancing at his chest—broad and sculpted, and rippling with muscles. And seeing his strong arms made me wonder what it would feel like to have him wrap them around me. . . .

Whoa! Wait a minute! I told myself. *What are you thinking? You have Alex.* And I had to stop looking at Scott, because I was totally staring.

"So what's up?" he asked lazily, folding his arms across his chest.

I shrugged. "Not much. How about with you?" *Good. This is good,* I told myself. *I don't sound like a freak who can't stop staring.*

He shrugged too.

"Want to go get some ice pops now, Jessica?" Megan asked.

"Uh, yeah. Sure." I allowed her and Maura to pull me away.

Scott stood back to let us pass, and then I heard him close the door to his room. The music got louder and louder, so that the bass was vibrating through the whole house.

Man, now I knew what Kerri was talking about. If I didn't have Alex, I'd be all over Scott Seifert in a heartbeat.

We all hung around on the backyard patio while Mr. Seifert and my dad made a big show of doing all the cooking. It was only hamburgers and hot dogs, but they kept kidding about special sauces and secret recipes like they were doing some Food Network TV show.

Mrs. Seifert and my mom were sitting at one end of the long picnic table, drinking gin and tonics from a pitcher. Mrs. Seifert spoke to Mom in a low voice, but I heard her say that they'd gone through most of their savings.

Megan and Maura and I sat in the grass, trying different outfits on their Barbie dolls. It was actually kind of fun.

After a while Mom and Mrs. Seifert left the table. They soon came back carrying bowls of salads. Dad and Mr. Seifert approached the table, each holding a platter of grilled meat.

We were filling our plates when Scott came out of the house with a beer in his hand, and wearing a T-shirt with the name of some New York bar scrawled across the front. He was really polite to my parents—he always had been—and he shook my father's hand and everything.

My parents were polite right back, but I saw them checking out the beer, and I knew what they were thinking.

We all sat at the picnic table. Megan and Maura scooted in on either side of me. Scott slid in across from us, next to my mother. While the twins chattered to me about some television show they never missed, I eavesdropped. My mom was asking Scott about school and New York.

He told her he was really bummed about leaving, but he was taking some classes at the University of Wisconsin while he was home, and working to save up money to go back to New York.

"Jessica's taking classes there too," my mother said.

Scott glanced at me. "I thought you were still in high school."

For some reason, I felt all flustered now that he was talking to me. "I am, but I'm in this special program that—"

"What classes are you taking?" he asked.

"Introduction to English Literature and Sociology 101."

"Intro to English Lit? Me too. We must be in different sections. Which instructor?"

"Diaz."

"Yeah? Me too. What do you think of her?"

"She's good," I said.

"Really? I think she sucks."

For a second I thought he was just being obnoxious, but then he started talking about what he didn't like about her, and he had some valid points. Maybe I didn't agree, but then, I hadn't taken any college courses before now. I couldn't make a comparison. Scott could. And did.

After dinner, the men went to look at the shed Mr. Seifert was building behind the garage. The women and Scott went into the house. The twins and I sat at the table dressing Barbies again.

Finally I told them I was going inside to see if our mothers needed any help with the dishes. I wandered through the kitchen, which was deserted, and grabbed a Snapple from the open cooler on the counter. Then, on my way through the dining room, I heard muffled crying.

The door to the small den off the living room was open, and when I looked through, I could see my mother and Mrs. Seifert. Mom had her arms around her. Mrs. Seifert was in tears, saying she didn't know what they were going to do.

My mom looked up and saw me through the crack in the door. We exchanged glances, and she motioned me away with one hand, patting Mrs.

Seifert's back with the other.

I walked on through the house and stepped out the front door, onto the porch. Scott was there, sitting on the glider. He was drinking another beer and rocking back and forth, staring straight ahead at some kids playing kickball in the street.

"Hey," he said, without turning his head to look at me.

"Hey," I said back.

I debated going back inside, but then he did turn, and he said, "So my mom's all bummed out, huh?"

I nodded.

"You know, this really sucks. My dad puts in twenty-five years with the bank, and it doesn't even matter in the end. He's out to make room for some new young guy with an MBA." He shook his head and took a giant swallow of beer. "That's why I'm never going to deal with the corporate world."

I didn't know what to say to that. I sat down on the steps and sipped my Snapple. Scott moved off the glider and sat on the step above mine. He leaned back on his elbows, his legs stretched straight out.

"It's too bad," I told him, feeling awkward. "It must have been really hard for you to leave school."

"Yeah, well, I had no choice. But I'm working so I can save some money, and I'm applying for financial aid too. . . . Hopefully I'll be back in New York by next semester."

"I want to go to NYU," I told him. "What's it like in New York?"

"Oh, man, I love it there," he replied. "Life in New York is really fast paced. In the daytime, people are always rushing to get somewhere, and at night, the bar and club scene is amazing." He paused a second. "You've got people coming from all over the world—just to live in that city, and everyone does their own thing, you know? Nobody cares if you're different. I had to leave a lot of good friends behind when I came back here."

"Sounds great," I said, but Scott didn't reply. "Um, do you have a girlfriend in New York?" I couldn't believe I said that, but suddenly, I really wanted to know.

He gave me this slow, sexy smile. "Not anymore. Why?"

I shrugged and tried to look bored. "Just curious."

He'd always had girlfriends, usually older than him and incredibly gorgeous.

"How about you? Got a boyfriend?" He rolled the beer bottle back and forth between his palms.

I gazed toward the street. "Kind of." A nervous flutter filled my stomach. *Why did I say that?* I wondered. *It isn't true. I do have a boyfriend.*

Scott made a little chuckling sound. "Kind of, huh?"

"Right." *Wrong. What are you doing, Jess?*

I heard Scott strike a match and turned to see him lighting a cigarette—a Marlboro.

"So you're taking classes at the university," he said, leaning back again and exhaling smoke.

"Only two courses—Soc 101 and English Lit." I knew I had already told him all that, but I was nervous.

I breathed in the secondhand smoke. Normally I thought it was a disgusting habit—I'd bugged my father about it for months until he finally went cold turkey a few years back. But for some reason, smoking seemed kind of sexy now that Scott was the one who was doing it. I watched as he took a deep drag, his eyes narrowing into that seductive squint.

I quickly looked away.

Dusk was falling, and it was getting chilly too. Now I wished I'd brought a jacket, or at least a sweatshirt. I thought I should probably go inside, but I didn't want to. I tilted my bottle and saw that there was nothing left in it but a few powdery, watery dregs.

"Why don't you go get a refill?" Scott suggested. "You can grab me another Molson while you're at it."

It's not exactly an order, I told myself as I got up.

32

It was more like an invitation.

The kitchen was dark, and through the window, I could see the four adults sitting on the patio in the backyard. A candle was lit in the center of the table, and from the light it cast on their faces, I saw that they were having a heavy discussion.

I grabbed two bottles of beer out of the cooler and searched through three drawers until I found an opener. I didn't really like beer, but there was no more Snapple—not that I'd looked very hard.

Back out on the porch again, I handed a beer to Scott and sat close beside him. I felt bold doing it— not to mention drinking beer right out in the open where my parents could see me and freak out. I guess I was willing to take chances tonight.

I thought about how Scott had always been this kind of distant figure. Older and, I don't know, I guess . . . dangerous. I'd grown up always hearing about how bad he was from my parents, but I was never exactly sure why they thought he was so horrible.

"What are you thinking about?" he asked me.

"Me? Nothing." I glanced up and met his gaze for a second, then quickly looked away. *Something is definitely happening between us,* I thought. Even though we were a few feet apart and not even looking at each other now, some kind of electrical current seemed to be zinging back and forth.

Scott reached into his pocket and took out another cigarette.

"Can I bum one?" I heard myself ask.

"Sure." Unfazed, he offered the pack.

Kerri and I used to sneak cigarettes at dances in middle school, but I'd never really liked it. I'd always known that I wouldn't be a smoker. Besides, the only girls who smoked were the ones with stringy hair who wore concert T-shirts and too much eye makeup. But right now, for some reason, I just wanted a cigarette.

Scott leaned over with a lit match. I placed the butt between my lips and took a long drag until it caught a glow.

"So where's your *kind of* boyfriend tonight?" Scott asked.

The lazy way he said it—and the way his arm seemed to accidentally brush along the length of mine as he leaned back—made my heart do a little cartwheel.

"Milwaukee," I said, my voice breaking a little.

Now his leg was right beside mine, his hip against mine, the whole length of our bodies just barely touching as we sat facing forward, not looking at each other.

"How come you didn't go?"

I shrugged, not knowing what else to do.

"Well, good thing you stayed home." He tossed his cigarette butt down and stubbed it out with his foot.

"Why?"

"Because . . ." Scott said. He turned to me, took the half-smoked cigarette out of my hand, and stubbed it out too.

For a moment we just stared at each other through the twilight, his eyes searching mine. I couldn't turn away or speak or even breathe.

Then Scott leaned over and kissed me.

Chapter 4

I closed my eyes and kissed Scott back. I kissed him back like crazy.

Scott was so different from Alex—nothing shy about his lips on mine, no caution in the way his strong arms pulled me toward him. His tongue slipped into my mouth as his hands drifted up my back and tangled in my long hair.

I let out a small moan. I hadn't been kissed like this since . . . since . . . ever.

But it was wrong. It was wrong because of Alex.

I broke off the kiss abruptly, and we just sat there for a moment. Scott gazed at me intensely. I felt like liquid in his arms, so weak I couldn't move if I wanted to.

And I didn't want to.

I wanted . . . I realized I didn't know what I wanted.

He started to kiss me again, and a little warning

bell went off in my head. No, not a little bell—a blaring siren, like for a five-alarm blaze. Summoning all my strength, I managed to utter one word.

"Stop." It came out sounding pathetic.

"How come?" he asked.

"Because I have a boyfriend."

"I thought you *kind of* have a boyfriend."

"He's more than that, Scott," I said, pulling away. "Actually, I've been with him for two years."

"Does he make you happy?"

I opened my mouth to say yes, but then I realized I wasn't so sure. *Did Alex make me happy? How come I never felt this turned on when he kissed me?* "He's a great guy," I said firmly.

Scott shrugged, as if he didn't believe me. "Can I ask you one more thing?"

"I guess so," I replied, bracing for another personal question.

"Do you have the notes from Friday's lit class? Because I cut, and I know Diaz is giving an essay test next week."

What? That's his question—after what just happened? I was so caught off guard that all I could do was stare at him.

"So . . . can I borrow them?" Scott asked.

This was it? We weren't going to discuss what had just happened between us, or my relationship with Alex, or anything?

"Um, sure," I replied, feeling a little let down.

"Great. I'll meet you tomorrow night so I can get them from you."

Tomorrow night, I thought. My heart began to beat faster. I really wanted to go, I realized. Then I remembered Alex. I looked at my watch. It was almost eight. I had to call Alex. "Can I use your phone?" I asked.

"Go ahead."

I went into the den and dialed Alex's number. He answered on the second ring.

"Hey, you're back," I said, trying to sound casual. Could he tell from my voice that I'd just kissed someone else?

"Yeah, I got in about an hour ago."

"How was it?"

"Great. How was your barbecue? Totally boring?"

"Totally," I said quickly. Too quickly, probably. I realized I couldn't see him tonight. Not so soon after that kiss. I needed time to think about everything.

"Listen, Alex, I don't think I can come over tonight. I'm still at the Seiferts. My parents want me to stay here for a while," I lied.

"That's okay. I'm really tired anyway."

I couldn't help feeling a little annoyed by that. I mean, we had plans. Shouldn't he be more eager to see me? Come to think of it, shouldn't I be disappointed that I wouldn't be seeing him? Well, I wasn't. Only relieved.

"I'm supposed to go to that student council thing tomorrow," he told me. "Amber wants to talk to me about putting a homecoming feature into the yearbook. You're going too, aren't you?"

"Yeah, but you don't have to go," I told him. "I'm the features editor. I can take care of it."

"It's no problem," Alex said. "Really. I want to do it."

Somehow that bugged me too. "Don't you think I can do my own job, Alex?"

"I just thought that since you have a lot of stuff going on, I'd help you out," Alex replied. "Why don't we go over together, okay?"

"Fine," I said. "I'll see you when I come back from my grandmother's house tomorrow. Bye, Alex." Then I hung up, and went back out to the porch.

Scott was still sitting there. It was definitely getting cool out, but it didn't seem to bother him.

"Hey again," I said, hugging my bare arms.

Scott stood up. "So can you meet me tomorrow night?" He moved closer, just a few inches away from me.

"Listen," I began. I wanted to tell him that I couldn't—that I had too many things to do. But for some reason, I really wanted to meet Scott, even if it was only to give him my notes. "Tomorrow night is no problem," I said.

Scott put his hand on my arm, and I quivered a little. "You're shivering, Jessica."

"Yeah, well, it was so warm out when we came over this afternoon I didn't think to bring a jacket, and now—"

He cut off the rest of my words with his mouth, lowering it over mine and kissing me again.

I pulled away. "Scott, no," I said firmly, even though I was secretly thrilled that he wanted me.

"Why not?" he asked.

"I told you. I have a boyfriend."

He smiled slightly, and I realized that it didn't make the least bit of difference to him. He bent toward me again, and just when I thought he was going to kiss my lips, he planted one on my forehead. "How about that? Is that okay?"

"Not really. I—"

"How about that?" He kissed my cheek.

"No, Scott, come on. Stop fooling around."

He put his arms around me, pulling me close. "Alright, then, Jessica. I'll just keep you warm, okay?"

I knew I should pull away, and believe me, I did. But not before I closed my eyes, and thought about how great it felt to know that this guy—who was totally hot—found me irresistible.

Sunday morning, I went to church with my parents and Ricky, and then to my grandmother's house for lunch. Everybody was there, as usual—my two aunts, three uncles, and a bunch of cousins, all of them younger than me. The oldest ones were in middle school, and the youngest was my aunt Angie's new baby, Michael. She let me hold him, and all I could think about was what Alex had said about how we had to be careful. As I stroked Michael's soft fuzzy head with one fingertip, I wondered what it would be like to have a baby. I don't know, maybe I'd even get to write about it one day.

After we got home, I ran up to my room to check my e-mail.

Hi, Jess,

Just got in from the movies with Matt. We saw the new Freddie Prinze one. I totally loved it. Matt hated it. But we both agreed that the pizza at the new place in the mall was awesome. You've got to try it with Alex. You'll be at the student council meeting this afternoon, won't you? I heard it's all about homecoming. Me, Maya, and Erin will pop down to Amber's to help make

posters for the fund-raiser, so we'll see you there.
    LYLAS, Kerri

Lately Kerri had begun signing her e-mails to me like that—Love You Like a Sister. It always made me smile.

The next e-mail was from Alex. I opened it.

Miss you! Hurry over as soon as you can.
    —Alex

Pushing back a wave of guilt, I turned off my computer and changed into jeans and a gray sweater. Then I grabbed my denim jacket and ran back downstairs.

"I'm going," I called in the direction of the living room, where my parents and Ricky were watching a football game.

I had planned on asking Dad to drop me off at Alex's, but now I felt like walking even though it was kind of far. I needed to think about what had happened between Scott and me.

Actually, ever since yesterday, that's all I'd been thinking about. My feelings swung from guilt—*How could I have cheated on Alex?*—to excitement—*I can't wait to see Scott again tonight*—to worry—*What will happen when I do see him again?*—to confusion—

What am I going to do?

I stopped at the 7-Eleven to get a Snapple. I put the bottle on the counter to pay, and fished through my bag for my wallet.

"That it?" asked the woman behind the counter.

"Yeah . . . uh, no." I had the sudden impulse to buy a pack of cigarettes. "Can I have a pack of cigarettes?" I said awkwardly. I felt my face instantly grow flaming hot.

The cashier looked at me with a raised eyebrow, as though she was waiting for something. "Well. . . ?"

Well, what? I thought, annoyed.

"What kind of cigarettes?" she asked in a slow, flat voice, as if she was going out of her way to be patient with me.

The two kids in line behind me snickered.

"Oh, sorry . . . Marlboro. Um, hard pack," I added significantly. I gave the kids a worldly glance over my shoulder.

The cashier reached above her head and pulled a red pack from the display, and tossed it onto the counter. "That it?"

"Matches." I paused. "And gum." I grabbed a pack of Bubble Yum from the bin in front of me and placed it on the counter.

I paid, then grabbed my little brown paper bag and raced out of the store. A few blocks away, I stopped, took out the pack of cigarettes, and opened it.

I stuck a cigarette between my lips and held it there for a few seconds, feeling sophisticated. I lit a match and touched it against the tip. The wind gusted up and the flame flared, burning my fingers. I yelped and dropped the cigarette.

This just wasn't working. What was I doing, smoking? What was I trying to prove? I thought I got over this in junior high. Guess not. I placed a second cigarette in my mouth.

I struck another match, held it to the tip, inhaled, and the cigarette lit up. It didn't taste as good as it had the other night, with Scott, but I kept it up.

So what am I going to do about Scott? I wondered, walking on down the street. *And what about Alex?*

I closed my eyes for a second and imagined Scott's kiss—the way he'd made me feel, the way I had kissed him back.

Break up with Alex. The thought totally took me by surprise.

But for a second, it seemed logical. After all, if I could feel so totally attracted to someone else, our relationship must be missing something, right?

On the other hand, I loved Alex. At least, I thought I did. And this was senior year. If Alex and I broke up, it would be pretty weird around school. Plus, what about homecoming and the prom? And working on the yearbook? What about my friends, who were all Alex's friends too?

Besides, the thing with Scott was really no big deal. Maybe it seemed like a big deal when I was with him. But now that I was away from him, I could see I was getting all worked up over practically nothing.

So I kissed a guy I've known forever, I thought. *Okay, he's older and very sexy. But I only kissed him a few times.*

So what, right?

As I came to Alex's corner, I threw the cigarette butt on the sidewalk and stomped it out. Then I stuck a piece of gum in my mouth, and made sure the pack of cigarettes was hidden in the inside pocket of my jacket. *I'm not going smoke any more of them, but it's a waste of money to just toss them,* I thought as I turned down Alex's street. *Maybe I'll give them to Scott later.*

Scott.

The thought of seeing him again sent a thrill through me.

This is not good, I decided, running up the steps to Alex's house. I knocked, and opened the door.

"Alex?" I called.

"Hi," he said, coming into the hall. He was wearing a navy sweater and a pair of jeans that looked like they'd just been ironed. He gave me a hug.

He smelled so good, like shampoo and fabric softener. And I felt totally guilty. I hugged him back extra hard. "I missed you yesterday," I said.

"Me too." He stared at me for a second. Was it my imagination or did he seem suspicious? It had to be my imagination. "I brought you something from Milwaukee," he said.

"You did?" More guilt. "What is it?"

He grabbed a plastic bag off the hall table, and handed it to me. I reached in and pulled out an adorable teddy bear.

"This is so cute, Alex," I said, feeling a huge lump rising in my throat. I felt as if I might choke—and I totally deserved it. Here was the sweetest boyfriend in the world, and I'd cheated on him.

"So are you," he replied, kissing the tip of my nose. Then he sniffed my hair. "You smell like smoke."

"That's because I just got back from my grandmother's house," I said immediately. Alex knew she smoked, and it wasn't really a lie. I did have lunch over there earlier.

"Wow, it's really strong." He wrinkled his nose. "Anyway, I tried to call you at home, but you'd already left."

"For what?"

"Nobody else is here, so I have to stay with Josh.

You go to the meeting without me. I'll leave as soon as my parents get back."

"All right. I'll see you there." I gave him a peck on the cheek, and hurried out with the teddy bear tucked under my arm.

Seeing Alex helped me make up my mind about Scott. Tonight was just going to be a platonic exchange of notes, and nothing more. *You and Alex are a couple,* I reminded myself. *And you love him . . .*

So why can't I stop thinking about Scott?

Chapter 5

A group of kids were hanging out in Amber's basement, where the meeting was about to take place. I spotted Kerri, Maya, and Erin sitting on an old couch, and joined them.

"Where's Alex?" Erin asked. "Isn't he supposed to talk about the yearbook or something?"

"He'll be here soon," I answered in a whisper as Amber Brawley, the class president, called for everyone to be quiet.

"First things first," Amber said. "Homecoming queen candidates will be nominated this week. The ballots are going around to homerooms. Anyone who's a homeroom rep should check with their teacher to make sure you have them."

Maya elbowed me. "This is your big chance, Jess."

She was right. Last year I'd been nominated for queen, and lost by three votes. If I got the nomination this year, I was planning to spend a lot more time on my essay. The teachers in our school didn't want Homecoming Queen to be a total popularity thing, so they made all the nominees write essays. The girl who wrote the best essay won. Good thing for me.

"I wish I could run," Kerri said. Cheerleaders weren't allowed to be homecoming queen. Another silly rule our school had. Again, with the popularity thing.

"You can't have everything, Ker," Erin said lightly.

About an hour later the meeting was winding up, and Alex still hadn't arrived. Amber looked at me. "Do you know where Alex is, Jessica?"

"He got hung up with something," I explained. "But I can talk to you about the homecoming feature if you want."

Amber shook her head. "No. Forget it," she said, and ended the official part of the meeting.

Then we split up into groups to make posters for the craft fair fund-raiser, which was the following week. My friends and I sprawled on the floor in a corner, surrounded by poster board and paints, and discussed our ideas.

Erin, our artist, had plans to tie-dye T-shirts. I thought it might be cool to sew up some triangle hair scarves, though I had no idea when I'd find the time to do it. Kerri couldn't decide between making friendship bracelets or beaded necklaces.

Maya was very quiet, though. I wondered why.

Then I noticed that Jimmy Wright and a couple of other basketball players were working on a poster nearby. I knew they all hung out with T.J., the guy who had practically attacked Maya, and I was glad he wasn't with them. Then I heard Jimmy whisper something to his friends, and they all laughed hysterically.

Maya glanced over her shoulder, then quickly turned away. She reached for a brush and accidentally knocked over an open jar of paint. "Oh, no!" she cried, jumping up. A huge yellow puddle spread across some poster board. "What a mess!"

"Hey, Maya, it's okay," Kerri said. "It didn't get on the floor or anything."

"Here's some paper towels," I said, handing her a roll.

Maya took them from me without a word. The tears in her eyes startled me. I didn't know what to say to her.

"Look at me," she said finally. "It's on my clothes. I have to go."

"You only have a drop on your sleeve," Erin said. "You can just clean it off in the bathroom. Come on, I'll help you," she offered.

"No, I really need to go," Maya told us. She kept her head down, staring at the floor. I could still hear

T.J.'s friends talking. I thought I heard one of them mention Maya's name.

I put an arm around her. "This isn't about paint, is it?"

Maya shrugged and looked at the floor again. "I really have to go," she said. "My dad's giving a speech later, and I need to change." She dropped the paper towels, grabbed her coat, and bolted out of Amber's basement, leaving the three of us to look at each other.

"I'm worried about her," I said.

"Maybe we should go over to her house later," Erin suggested.

"I can't," I said unhappily.

"How come?" Kerri asked.

I hesitated. *What would they think of me if I told them about Scott?* Then I took a deep breath. *No. They're my closest friends. I could use their advice.* "I have to—"

"Shhh!" Kerri elbowed me. "Listen."

"Yeah, I'm sure it was Maya Greer," Jimmy told his friends. "She did it with T.J. at Turtle Donovan's party. She didn't even know T.J., but that didn't matter to her."

"Yeah, I heard she was all over him," someone else said.

"She did *what?*" Kerri asked sharply, turning around.

"What do you think?" Jimmy said smugly.

Erin rose and stepped toward them. "That's a total lie," she said hotly. Kerri and I stood too, and faced Jimmy and his friends.

"Yeah, shut up, Wright," Luke Perez said. He was standing apart from the others.

"How do you know, Perez?" another basketball player asked.

"Give me a break!" Kerri cried before Luke could answer. "Maya would never do something like that. You have no idea what you're talking about."

Jimmy was about to speak when Luke stepped forward. "Don't even think about saying anything else about Maya," he said, staring him down.

"Okay, okay." Jimmy said, raising his hands. He glanced from Kerri to Luke and back to Kerri.

"This rumor about Maya is really getting out of hand," Erin whispered after a few tense moments. "I feel terrible for her."

"No wonder she ran out of here," I said, going back to my painting. "I didn't realize it was so bad."

"The problem is, there's nothing we can do about it," Erin said. "Except stick up for her."

"It'll die down as soon as they find someone else to talk about," Kerri assured us. "I'm more worried about Maya. She's really freaking out about what happened with T.J."

"No kidding." I picked up a new paintbrush and dipped it into some orange paint. "Maybe she'll feel like talking later. I'll give her a call tonight."

"Me too," Erin said.

"I wish she'd call that helpline number I gave her," Kerri said. "I mean, we can all try to talk to her about it, but a counselor could really help. Maya's got a lot to deal with."

I knew Kerri was right, but I still planned on calling Maya.

"So how was that barbecue at the Seiferts' yesterday, Jess?" Kerri asked me suddenly. "Was Scott there?"

She caught me off guard. I looked up at her, and then at Erin, and I felt my cheeks burning.

"What?" Kerri asked, and by the way she was looking at me, I could tell she knew something was up.

"You're totally blushing," Erin added. "Spill it, Jess."

"It's just . . . yeah, Scott was there."

Kerri studied me. "Something happened between you two." It wasn't even a question. When people had been friends as long as we had, there wasn't much you could hide.

"I didn't mean for anything to happen with Scott." I dipped my brush into the paint so hard that it spattered onto the poster. I didn't even bother to wipe it off. "Like, it was totally unplanned."

"*What* was totally unplanned?" Kerri practically shrieked. "What did you do with him, Jess?"

"Not so loud, Kerri." I glanced around the room. "We didn't do anything. I mean, it wasn't any big deal or anything. We . . . um, I just kissed him," I replied, shrugging—a *no big deal* kind of shrug.

"Wow," Kerri said. "Scott Seifert. I can't believe you did that, Jess."

"What about Alex?" Erin asked, her eyes open wide.

"I love Alex, but . . ." I shook my head. "I don't know. . . . I don't know what I'm doing."

"Don't stress over it." Erin touched my arm. "It was only one kiss, right?"

I shook my head, sheepishly. "More than one."

"So, tell us how it was!" Kerri said excitedly.

"Incredible," I confessed. "I mean, you guys . . . he is so hot, and he has this way of, oh, I don't know, making you feel like he totally wants you."

"And Alex doesn't?" Erin questioned gently. "I thought you two were really into each other."

"So did I," I told her, glad that I was able to talk this through with them. "It's just that Alex is so . . ."

"Nice," Kerri added knowingly.

I nodded. He was nice. A really great guy. I took a deep breath and stared at my friends. "I thought

Alex was everything I wanted—until Scott kissed me."

"Are you going to see him again?" Kerri asked.

"Tonight. I'm giving him notes for a class we both have," I said. "But it's not a date," I added quickly.

"Would you go out with Scott if he asks you?" Erin wanted to know.

"I'm not sure," I admitted, feeling sort of sick inside. I didn't want to be thinking about seeing another guy—but I was. "I just don't want to hurt Alex."

"We know," Kerri said. "But maybe the only way you'll be able to tell if you and Alex really belong together is if you go out with Scott, like once or something."

"Just be careful," Erin told me. "College guys probably move a lot faster than high school ones."

I thought about Maya again, and what had happened between her and T.J. Part of me just wanted to hide, to forget all about Scott and the way he made me feel.

The other part couldn't wait until tonight.

Chapter 6

Back in my room, I sat on my white canopy bed with my lighted makeup mirror set up on the patchwork quilt that my grandmother had made for me. I had the new issue of **seventeen** propped open in my lap, and I was experimenting with a new eye makeup look that the magazine described as "smoldering." It involved lots of shadow, charcoal pencil, and mascara, and smudging the makeup around the eye with a Q-tip.

Next I tried on lipsticks until my mouth looked exactly like the model's on the magazine cover, kind of soft and pouty. Sort of French, I thought. I straightened my long wavy hair until it was very sleek and shiny. Then I sat back and checked out the results.

Fabulous. I didn't look like Jessica Carvelli, high school girl, anymore. I looked older. Prettier. Sexier. I felt happily rebellious just thinking about what my mother would say when she saw me. No less, if I went to school looking like this tomorrow.

Now for some clothes. I slipped into my sister Lisa's room and opened her closet door. Sure enough, there was plenty of stuff left on the wire hangers, all of it black. Jackets and pants and skirts and tops. I grabbed an armload of stuff and raced back to try it all on.

Finally I found an outfit to go with my new look—short black suede skirt, a rib-hugging sweater, and knee-length black boots. I put on some hoop earrings and a bracelet I hardly ever wore, then stepped back to examine the full effect in the mirror.

"Wow," I muttered under my breath. I was barely recognizable. I knew I could get away with this to meet Scott tonight—but what about for school tomorrow?

For a second, I imagined that Alex would see me in the hall, and his knees would get all weak, and he'd grab me and kiss me passionately.

Then reality took over, and I knew he'd hate it.

But that didn't matter. Because in the back of my mind it wasn't really Alex I wanted to impress.

It was Scott.

I wanted him to think I was just as sophisticated and sexy as any college girl. I wanted him to think I was irresistible, the way he did last night. I couldn't pretend, even to myself, that I didn't.

I paced back and forth on the tree-lined sidewalk, glancing in the shop windows along State Street. When I reached the corner, I checked my watch. Scott had said to meet in front of Starbucks on the corner of State and Gilman at seven.

But he was late. So late that I started to wonder whether I'd missed him, or whether we'd gotten our signals crossed, or if he'd just decided not to show up.

I leaned against a mailbox, and watched some kids from another high school hanging out in the little park across the street. One of them had a boom box, and turned up the volume when an old Beastie Boys song came on.

Should I call Scott's house? I wondered. *No, I'd better not. If I did, and his parents or sisters answered, they'd wonder what was up.*

And then my parents would probably find out I was meeting Scott, and I'd never hear the end of it. All the way home from the Seiferts' the other night, they'd talked about his appearance and outspoken politics and general attitude problem. So, as much as I hated to lie, I'd told them I was going to the library on campus to finish studying for my sociology test tomorrow.

"Hey, Jessica!"

I turned and saw Scott coming toward me. Not striding briskly, like someone who was late, but sauntering along, wearing his lazy grin.

"Hi!" I said, forgiving him on the spot for making me wait.

I caught his eyes flicking up and down over me. I'd thrown on Lisa's old black peacoat but left it unbuttoned. His gaze seemed to linger below my neck, as if he was wondering what I looked like without the coat. I kind of liked that.

"Got the notes?" he asked, his eyes moving back to my face.

"The notes," I repeated, blank for a second. Then . . . "Oh, my God! The notes!" How mortifying. I'd been so psyched to see him again that I'd totally forgotten the reason we were meeting.

Scott looked amused. "Hey, it's okay. I'll get them from you tomorrow."

"No, I can go back home and—"

"Don't do that. I'll get them tomorrow."

"But I thought you needed them."

"You know what I need? Some food. I'm in the mood for sushi," he said, and pointed to a place a few doors down the street. "Let's go get some."

"Sushi?" I echoed weakly, falling into step beside him. "Sushi is raw fish, isn't it?"

"You'll love it," he assured me. "And by the way . . ." He cast me a sideways glance as we crossed the street. "You look incredible, Jess."

"Oh?" I tried desperately to keep my mouth from curving into a smile. "Thanks. So do you."

"That was really good," I told Scott as we left the sushi place.

"I told you you'd like it."

"I can't believe I ate eel and octopus."

"Yeah, but you didn't try the tuna. The tuna is the best."

"It was just too . . . red." I shuddered at the thought of it. "Maybe next time."

"Next time?" Scott caught my eye. "So we're going out again?"

I glanced away. "We're not going out," I said, shoving my hands into the pockets of my jacket.

For the past hour, I had sat two feet away from Scott trying to deny that I was crazy about him—that all I wanted was for him to lean over and kiss me like he did the night before. I even forgot to worry about what we'd talk about. Not that it mattered. Somehow we both had a lot to say.

"Look," Scott began, "I know you have a boyfriend—"

"Alex," I said, hoping that saying his name out

loud would conjure up an image of his face, because suddenly, I couldn't even remember what he looked like.

"Whatever," Scott said. "I'm not really looking for a girlfriend. But that doesn't mean we can't hang out together and, you know . . ."

"I know. . . . No, I don't. What?" I looked up at him.

"This." We both stopped walking, and he slipped his hands around my waist.

The next thing I knew Scott was kissing me.

My stomach flipped as he pulled me closer. My head swirled at the intensity of his touch. I was floating. Floating above us. Seeing two passionate lovers embrace in the middle of a crowded sidewalk. Their lips entwined. Their bodies wanting each other.

Scott gazed at me as I reluctantly pulled away. I wanted it to keep going. I wanted more than kissing. I felt this huge aching inside, way more powerful than anything I'd ever felt with Alex.

"Wow," I said, trying to regroup.

"So I'll see you again, right?" Scott asked.

All I could do was nod, against my better judgment.

I was still a little shaken when I got home, and I went straight to my room. I knew that I should probably study for my sociology test, but there was

no way I was going to be able to concentrate. Instead
I turned on my computer to check my e-mail:

> Jess,
> What's happening? How did it go with Scott?
> Alex got to Amber's right after you left. I told him
> you went to the mall with your mom. I didn't want
> him calling you at home when you were out with
> Scott. Hope I did the right thing. E me back with
> all the details.
> Love, Erin

Thanks, Erin, I thought, and moved on to the
next one:

> Spill it, girlfriend! How was your date with
> Mr. Hot? I'm glad I'm not in your shoes. As crazy
> as I am about Matt—I don't know what I'd do if a
> hottie like Scott came my way. E-mail me as soon
> as you get home, I'm dying to know.
> LYLAS, Kerri

I hit Reply, figuring I'd send one e-mail back to
both of them:

> Scott and I had a great time. I didn't exactly
> tell him I didn't want to see him anymore. Instead

we kissed again. The problem is that when I'm with him I feel so . . .

I stopped there. *How did I feel when I was with Scott?* I wasn't sure how to put it into words.

Sighing, I sat back in my chair. I didn't know what to tell them. *Maybe I'll know after I think about things some more.* I deleted the e-mail I'd written. *I'll see them in school tomorrow, anyway. Hopefully I'll have things sorted out by then.*

I clicked on the third e-mail:

Erin told me you had to go to the mall with your mom, so I didn't bother calling you at home. Listen, I wanted to remind you that your yearbook article ideas are due tomorrow. See you then.
—Alex

I checked the time. It was late. I really needed to finish studying for sociology before I tackled the yearbook stuff. Maybe I should get up early and write up my article ideas before school. That might work out. And if I didn't have them, well, Alex would understand.

I opened my sociology textbook and started to read.

Poor, Alex. He'd never know that slacking off on my yearbook work was the very least of it.

Chapter 7

I felt like a different person the next day as I drove myself to school in my mom's car—a little more confident, I guess. I turned up the music on the radio, and slipped on my black sunglasses.

I had decided to go for it with my new look, and wore a snug black V-neck top that showed a little cleavage. Actually, I didn't even realize I had cleavage until I borrowed one of Lisa's Wonderbras. I was just glad that I hadn't seen my parents or Ricky this morning. I stayed in my room until my parents left for work, and Ricky caught a ride to school with his friends. I knew I was going to have to break them into my new look slowly.

I stopped at a red light, and glanced in the rearview mirror to check my hair and makeup. Same as last night. I looked pretty hot, if I did say so myself.

When I caught sight of the huge red building

that was my school, I felt a little flutter in my stomach. *What is Alex going to say when he sees me?* I wondered, pulling into a spot in the crowded parking lot. I shook the thought away, got out of the car, and headed toward school.

"Who is that?" I heard a guy ask. He was part of a group of boys leaning against the wall in front of the school entrance.

I smiled to myself. I kind of felt like Olivia Newton-John at the end of *Grease*, where she blew everyone away with her new look at that school carnival.

"Isn't that Ricky Carvelli's sister?" Another guy asked. "I never knew she was so . . ." The last part I didn't hear.

They were totally staring at me as I walked passed them. Now I wished they'd stop gawking, and I tugged up my sweater a little. All this attention was kind of making me self-conscious.

Finally I made it into the school. The greasy security guard looked me up and down, and shot me a toothy grin as I passed him. *Ew,* I thought, feeling the sudden urge to take a shower. *I wanted guys to notice me, but I didn't mean him.*

I pushed through a swinging door, and marched up the stairwell to my locker at the very end of the second floor. I was almost there when I heard Maya's voice behind me. "Jessica!"

I turned around. Maya, Kerri, and Erin were rushing over. "Hi, guys," I said, smiling.

"What's with the boobs?" Kerri asked as soon as they were close enough.

"Nothing." I felt my face grow hot. "I just thought I'd try something new."

"I didn't even recognize you," Erin said, lifting a strand of my hair.

"So this is the new you," Kerri said, smiling, "now that you've gone out with a college guy?"

"We didn't go out," I reminded her.

"I thought you were just giving Scott your notes," Maya chimed in. "Kerri and Erin filled me in last night."

"Oh," I said, suddenly realizing what a jerk I was. I had made a big deal about calling Maya yesterday, and I was the only one who hadn't done it. I started to feel bad about not returning Kerri's and Erin's e-mails too.

"Well, I think you look awesome!" Erin chirped. "I'd say you could pass for, like, at least twenty-five."

"Really?" I brightened.

"Totally," Kerri said. "Alex is going to love it—even if he's used to the wholesome look. But you know . . ." Kerri trailed off. A little smirk crossed her lips.

"What?" I asked her, bracing myself.

"Well . . . are homecoming queens even allowed to wear Wonderbras? I mean, it might hurt your chances for a nomination."

Erin and Maya cracked up.

I gave them a look—one that said, "Who cares?" "Spare me the next time, okay?"

Maya and Kerri glanced at each other.

I decided to ignore them, and checked the clock on the wall. "I've got to get to homeroom. I'll see you guys later."

"Right, later," Kerri agreed. "At chorus. You can tell us more about Scott."

"Can't," I said. "I'm skipping it. I have to get over to campus early to go over my notes before my test. I'm sure Mr. Calvert will understand."

"Oh." Now Kerri traded a glance with Erin.

"But I'll be back for that extra chorus practice after school," I quickly pointed out. All four of us had been chosen to be in a special group that was performing a cappella at the Christmas concert in December.

"Fine. We'll talk then," Kerri said. Then she, Maya, and Erin took off down the hall together, leaving me to wonder about the looks they had exchanged.

In all my life, I'd never gotten so much attention from the male population. Everywhere I went that morning, some guy was checking me out and saying "Hi, Jess," like we were old friends.

I didn't exactly get how makeup and clothes could make a difference in the way guys treated me, but they did. They made a huge difference. And I knew that if I thought about it long enough, I'd probably decide that was insulting. So I didn't think about it anymore.

I ran into Alex right before third period. I was rushing toward my locker to drop off some books. Then I would head to the university.

His jaw dropped when he saw me coming down the hall. "Jessica, what are you doing?" he asked in a hushed tone as soon as I was beside him.

Instant irritation. "What do you mean, what am I doing? I'm going to my locker."

"I mean, what's all . . ." He gestured wildly with his hand.

"What's all *what*, Alex?" Suddenly, I couldn't stand him. Scott didn't have a problem with my new look. Compared to him, Alex seemed so . . . wholesome. So . . . *high school*.

"Why are you dressed like that? What are you trying to do, pick up guys? I mean, you look . . ."

I narrowed my eyes, daring him. If ever I felt like picking a fight, it was now.

"You don't look like you," he finished lamely.

"So? Maybe I'm tired of looking like me," I said, clutching my notebook across my chest, feeling a little self-conscious.

"Why? I think you're pretty. This way, you seem . . ." He trailed off and shrugged.

"Whatever, Alex. I can change my style if I want to, okay?"

He didn't know what to say to that. A few kids had sort of paused on their way to class, trying to listen.

"I just liked you better the old way," he muttered.

"Well, I'm sorry, but I like me better this way," I told him, even though I wasn't sure that was the truth. It was just that right now I was so angry with him—maybe more angry than I had a right to be. I couldn't help wondering why. "I have to get to campus," I said finally.

"Now?" Alex asked. "You're cutting chorus?"

I sighed. "Do you have a problem with that too?"

Alex raised his hands in defense. "No, I just . . . look, good luck on your test. I'll call you after school to see how it went."

"Okay." I turned to leave. "Bye."

"Hey, Jess?" he called as I started to walk away. "Did you hand in that yearbook stuff to the adviser?"

Oh, God, I thought. *Now I totally don't have a reason to be angry at Alex. I completely forgot to get up to write out my ideas. I didn't have anything to turn in. Not a scrap.*

But I didn't want to tell him that. "I left it out in the car," I said. "I'll get it and put it in your mailbox in the yearbook office." Then I raced out of the building.

Does Alex know I was lying to him? I wondered as I got into the car and drove to the university. I felt a pang of disappointment in myself, but I had to shake it off. I had to focus on college now.

I parked in the commuter lot on campus, and took the long way to the student union. As I climbed up Bascom Hill, I gazed at the liberal arts buildings and the beautiful old trees that were just starting to change color.

I stared at the guys walking in front of me. They were both wearing shorts and fraternity sweatshirts, even though there was a chill in the air. One of them swung his backpack as he described the awesome party he'd been to over the weekend. And I realized that I couldn't wait to go to college full-time.

The student union was buzzing with activity, with people eating lunch and joking around. It seemed as though everyone knew at least one person—everyone except me.

I guess I was a little shyer in college than I was in high school—probably because I'm younger than everybody. I added a note to my mental checklist—

right under ace sociology test—*get over being shy in college. Fast.*

But first things first. I bought a yogurt, and sat at an empty table to go over my notes. When I was finished, I hurried to my sociology class, mentally quizzing myself for the exam.

I noticed a guy leaning against the wall outside the lecture hall. *Scott!* I guess I *did* know one person in college after all.

I took in a sharp, excited breath and pretended to scan my open notebook, acting as if I didn't see him.

"Hey, Jess," he said as I walked closer.

Fake surprise, I told myself. *Like you didn't notice him till he called your name.* I glanced up. "Oh, hi! What's up?"

"Not much. What's up with you?"

He looked fantastic in faded, threadbare Levi's and a beat-up flannel shirt. And oh, my God, the way he was staring at me . . . I just wanted to break out into a big smile.

No. Stay calm, Jess. I bit my lip. "Nothing," I said. "I have those notes if you want them."

"No. Don't worry about it," Scott replied. He stared into my eyes. "Jess, I've been thinking about last night."

"You have?" My heartbeat sped up.

"Haven't you?" His voice was low.

"I guess I have too," I confessed, trying to keep cool.

"So when are we going out again?" he asked.

"Don't know," I replied. I was getting good at this.

"Meet me after class, okay?" Scott touched my arm. The feel of his warm fingers against my skin was electrifying.

"After class?" I squeaked. All my good intentions evaporated, and I gave him a big geeky smile.

But what about Alex? a voice screamed inside my head. *It's not fair to him.* I knew that already. Why did I have to keep reminding myself? Then I remembered something else—chorus practice. I had to get back to school.

"Listen, Scott." I paused and took a deep breath. He was so hard to resist. "I want to, but I can't."

"Boyfriend?" he asked.

"Um . . . chorus," I told him. "I'm in this special group—I had to audition for it and everything, so it's kind of important that I be there."

Just then two pretty sorority types walked by, and I noticed them staring at Scott. They didn't even try to hide their interest, actually turning their heads to check him out. Then they whispered to each other and giggled after they passed us.

That did it. Here I was with this impossibly

gorgeous guy, and he actually liked me. Me! And I was telling him I couldn't meet him because of chorus practice. What an idiot!

Scott turned his head and watched the two girls walk away, making me feel uncertain . . . and jealous. He glanced at his watch before turning back to me.

"I have to go," I blurted out nervously. "I've got to take a test."

"Yeah, I should get to class too," he said, gazing off down the hallway. It was crowded—kids were sitting on benches and standing around in little groups, talking and laughing and calling out to people they knew.

All at once I was overwhelmed with the feeling that I didn't belong here. Everyone else was older than me—they were away from home, living in dorms, going to classes full-time. I was an outsider, a little high school kid playing dress-up.

"Okay, well . . ." Scott glanced over his shoulder toward the stairs.

He's not brushing me off, he's just distracted, I told myself, but I didn't really believe it. I was getting ready to tell him I'd skip chorus practice when this sophomore girl, Bree, showed up. She was in my sociology class, and usually sat behind me, but we'd never really spoken before.

I saw her look Scott over, then glance at me in

surprise. I wondered if she was caught off guard by my new appearance or by the fact that someone like him was talking to someone like me.

"Hey," she said. "Jessica, isn't it?"

I nodded.

"You're the one who's in high school, right?" she added.

I wanted to cringe. Our professor, Dr. Krieger, had dropped that little tidbit of information in front of the whole class the first day.

"Yeah, that's me," I said, wishing I looked like her. She had sleek dark hair cropped really short and a beautiful face with superhigh cheekbones.

"Did you study for the exam?" Bree asked me.

"Pretty much," I replied.

Bree looked at me, then Scott, then back at me.

"Oh," I said. "Bree, this is Scott. Scott, Bree."

He flashed her a smile as he said hello, and I couldn't help feeling kind of jealous again.

"So listen," I said to Scott, knowing Bree was soaking up every word, "we never figured out when we're going out again."

"Oh, right. We didn't, did we?" If he was surprised by my sudden change of attitude, he didn't show it. "How about tomorrow night?" he suggested.

"Sounds good to me," I said.

"Fine. I'll call you later, Jess." He smiled and

stared deeply into my eyes. Then he said good-bye, barely glancing at Bree.

I watched him walk away, my heart pounding.

"How did you meet *him?*" Bree asked. I had almost forgotten she was there.

"Oh, he's an old friend," I told her, trying to sound casual.

"Cool." She glanced at me, looking impressed as we walked into the lecture hall together. For the first time, I almost felt like I had made a friend in college.

I mean, in high school, I had plenty of friends. I never went anywhere solo—from class to class, or even to my locker. Not unless I wanted to.

Here, I was pretty much a loner, and it wasn't because I wanted it to be that way. Now, with Bree beside me, I felt a little different—more like I fit in.

I knew she had only noticed me because of Scott. But torn as I was, going out with him was starting to feel more and more like the right move.

Chapter 8

"Time's up, Ms. Carvelli," Dr. Krieger said as I scribbled down the last sentence of my sociology essay. He was standing over me, waiting to collect my exam booklet.

The test had been hard, a lot harder than I thought it would be. I was one of the last people to finish, and I left the lecture hall feeling sort of drained and with a bad case of writer's cramp.

"You look like you can use some coffee," Bree said as I walked out of the class and into the hall.

"Tell me about it," I replied, still pondering over how poorly I thought I did on the exam.

"Let's go to the student union." Bree slung an arm around my shoulders. "We can hang out, get something to eat, trash Dr. Krieger. . . . "

I laughed. "We're there," I told her. "But I can't stay too long."

The union was noisy and sprawling with college

students, eating and hanging out. Bree and I sat near a huge picture window that had a view of the terrace off Lake Mendota. We had a great time getting to know each other, and commenting on the guys outside playing football and Frisbee by the water.

"Time check," I said, glancing at my watch. I gasped. It was 2:35. "Mr. Calvert's going to kill me!" I gathered my books. "If I leave now, I'll only be fifteen minutes late for practice."

I waved good-bye to Bree, and raced back to South Central. I burst into the auditorium, breathless. Everyone else was already on the risers, holding their sheet music. "Sorry I'm late," I panted.

Mr. Calvert stood in front of the chorus, holding his baton. "No problem, Jessica. You just made it."

I was glad Mr. Calvert was being so laid back about this. With my sheet music in hand, I hopped onto the risers next to Kerri. She and I were altos. Erin and Maya shot me questioning looks from the soprano section.

Then our teacher tapped his baton on his music stand, and we began singing. Erin had a solo in the middle. She has a powerful voice, and when she was finished, I fought the urge to applaud her. I smiled and gave her a thumbs-up as we finished the piece.

"Nice job, everyone. And Erin, that was fantastic," Mr. Calvert said. "I can tell you've been practicing."

She nodded, suddenly looking kind of shy. "Thanks, Mr. C."

"All right, let's work on the Gershwin piece next. I have some copies of the second verse in my office. Take a quick break and I'll be right back."

As Mr. Calvert left the room. Kerri and I wandered over to the soprano section.

"Hey, Maya, how did your dad's speech go yesterday?" I asked.

"Boring, as always." She was trying to sound casual, but she looked upset. Then she glanced over my shoulder, and I turned around to check it out. I realized she wasn't upset about her father's boring speeches. T.J. Miller was striding toward us.

He could have walked around us, but he purposely got right into Maya's face. "'Scuse me, ladies," he said in this fake polite, totally smug way.

Why was he doing this to her? I wondered. Why couldn't he just leave Maya alone? I let out a heavy breath, trying to hold my tongue. I knew if I said something right now, it would probably make the situation worse. I glanced at Kerri. I could tell she was probably thinking the same thing.

Maya tried to ignore T.J. She turned her back and looked at her shoes.

"How's it goin', Maya?" T.J. asked, taking another step forward and singling her out.

"Leave me alone," she mumbled.

"What's wrong?" he said, in mock dismay. "You're acting almost as if you don't like me."

"She doesn't like you, T.J.," Kerri muttered. "In fact, none of us like you."

"I know you're not the brightest crayon in the box," Erin added. "But even you should have figured that out by now."

"Really?" T.J. asked, surprised. "That's not how it seemed at Turtle's party. She couldn't get enough of me. Right, Maya?"

Maya looked as if she was about to cry. "You're a liar!" she burst out. "You make me sick, T.J.!"

"I think you're the one who's lying," T.J. said, turning to one of his friends. "Isn't she, Jimmy?"

I looked to see Jimmy Wright, the basketball player who was talking about Maya yesterday at Amber's house.

"I wasn't there, but I heard all about it," Jimmy said. "Sounds to me like she's the one lying."

"Give me a break! How can you believe anything he says?" I spoke up, poking T.J. in the arm.

"Hey, I couldn't make up something that good," T.J. said.

"You're disgusting!" Maya cried. She made a choking sound, and took off out the door. She bumped into Mr. Calvert on the way out.

"Maya? What's the matter?" he called. "Hey, Maya, wait!"

Erin rushed down to the front of the room. She whispered something to the teacher, and I saw him look doubtfully out the door where Maya had disappeared. Then he closed it.

Erin returned to the risers looking grim. As she passed me and Kerri, heading back to her spot, she said, "I told him to let her leave—that she was going to the bathroom to hurl."

I nodded, and stared down at my sheet music, unable to read the notes. All I could think about was Maya. "We should go after her," I whispered to Kerri. But then Mr. Calvert lifted his baton to start us in the next song. *I'll stop by her house on my way home,* I decided.

As Mr. Calvert gave some special instructions to the soprano section, Kerri leaned toward me. "Let's go to Maya's house right after this," she whispered.

"You just totally read my mind," I whispered back.

Mr. Calvert tapped his baton, and the room went silent. All heads faced forward.

I found my place in the Gershwin piece, thinking the sooner we sang, the sooner we could get out of there. All of my own problems seemed sort of petty now. Maya needed us, and we had to be there for her.

• • •

"Busy signal," Kerri said, hanging up the pay phone outside the auditorium. "Maybe she's online. She could be tied up for hours."

"Or maybe she took the phone off the hook," Erin said. "You know the way Maya gets when she's upset. She doesn't want to talk to anybody."

"Let's just go there," I said.

We walked out to my mom's car, and silently rode to Maya's house near Lake Monona. I pulled up the circular drive, right in front of the majestic home. Maya and her family had moved here from Kensington Heights about three years ago.

We were all really impressed the first time we saw the huge place with its stately pillars and sprawling green lawns. Then Maya pointed out that the shrubs circled the entire house, and kind of reminded her of a moat. That's when we all started calling her house *the castle*—and we've been doing it ever since.

As soon as I parked, Kerri jumped out of the car, ran up the steps to the wide porch, and pushed the doorbell. Erin and I followed.

I was surprised when Maya answered the door. I guessed that their housekeeper, Betty, must be gone for the day.

"Oh, hi, guys," she said, sounding surprised to see us. "What are you doing here?"

"We just wanted to stop by and see how you were," I said.

"We thought maybe you wanted some company," Erin added. "You know, if you felt like talking about . . . oh, hey, Mr. Greer," Erin said suddenly. I glanced over her shoulder, catching sight of Maya's father. He was sitting in the family room in front of the computer. He waved.

"My dad came home early today," Maya explained. "He's speaking tonight at the Rotary Club. I'm going too, so I need to get ready. I don't really have time to talk."

"That's okay, Maya," I said. "I'll call you or send you an e-mail tonight."

"Me too," Kerri said.

"Ditto," Erin added. "And don't worry. We'll help you figure something out."

"Thanks, guys." Maya looked at each of us and finally smiled. A real smile, I mean. "I'll catch you later then."

We quickly said good-bye, then piled back into my mom's car. I wished we could have talked to Maya, but at least she knew we were thinking about her.

I dropped off Kerri first, then swung by Erin's house, which was right around the corner from my house.

When we pulled up, Erin's neighbor, Glen Daley, was sitting on her front steps. "What's he doing here?" I asked, a little disappointed. I kind of wanted to spend some time with her—to sort of make up for the times I hadn't been around.

"Oh," Erin said. "We're supposed to check out college websites on my computer this afternoon. No big deal."

We got out of the car, and Glen walked toward us.

I liked Glen. Everybody did. He was really into art, like Erin, and he wanted to be a filmmaker, which I thought was cool. I always told him maybe someday I'd write a book and he could turn it into a movie.

"Come on in, guys," Erin said, leading us into her house.

"Sorry I was late getting back," Erin said to Glen. "We had stop at Maya's after chorus practice."

"That's okay," Glen said with a shrug. "I wasn't waiting long."

"Come on in the kitchen. I'll get us some soda and chips," Erin offered. Glen happily trailed after her, but I was kind of feeling like a third wheel.

"Listen, I really can't hang out," I said, hoping to make a quick escape. "It's late. I need to get home and do some stuff before supper."

Glen seemed to perk up when he heard that. I realized he wasn't so thrilled to see me either.

"Sure," Erin said. "Listen, I just want to give you that CD I told you about the other day. It's really good studying music." She walked over to the stereo on the family room wall unit and rummaged through a stack of CDs.

Glen followed her. "Who's the band?" he asked, sounding interested.

"Error Message," Erin said, flipping through the CDs.

"I've never heard of them," Glen said.

"They're really great," Erin replied. "I saw them with Keith last summer." Keith was the guy she'd fallen for while she was in Seattle visiting her aunt Joyce. Glen's face fell at the mention of his name.

Erin had her back turned and didn't see the way he cringed when she went on. "Keith is really into jazz. He says this band is influenced by some of the all-time greats. He says they're going to break into the mainstream music scene any second now."

"Yeah, well, you never know," Glen said. He sat down on the couch and folded his arms across his chest.

He has a major crush on Erin, I realized, which was really weird. Well, maybe not so weird since the two of them had been friends forever. The question was, why didn't Erin get it? Or maybe she did, and all this talk about Keith was just to send him a message. I'd have to ask her about it some other time.

Erin found the CD and handed it to me. "Thanks, I'll give this a try," I said, heading for the door. "Bye, Erin. See you, Glen."

They both said good-bye, and I left for home. As I drove through the twilight, I thought that Erin and Glen would make a cute couple. Maybe I should bring it up to her. Then again, maybe I shouldn't. She was really determined to keep the long-distance relationship going with Keith, and I didn't want to confuse her. I knew firsthand what it was like to be mixed up about guys, and it wasn't exactly what I would call fun.

My father's car wasn't in the driveway when I got back, but somebody had turned on the lamp in the living room. That meant my mother was home. Her friend Anne, who worked at the same insurance company, dropped her off now that I needed her car on weekdays.

I stepped into the house and wiped my shoes on the mat.

"Jessica? Is that you?"

"Yeah, Mom."

"Alex is on the phone for you," she said. I walked into the kitchen, and she handed me the cordless, barely glancing at me. I was waiting for her to say something about my new look, but I guess she hadn't noticed.

"Hey," I said into the receiver.

Alex didn't say anything back, and I knew that something was wrong. He let out a long sigh. "Jessica, did you think I wouldn't find out about this?"

Chapter 9

"**F**ind out?" I echoed, clutching the phone. "Find out about what?"

"Think about it," he said.

I did. I thought about all of the things that I'd done lately that could possibly make Alex angry. My head started to hurt.

"The yearbook features ideas," Alex said after a few seconds of silence. "You never handed them in."

I sighed in relief. "Oh, God. Sorry, Alex."

"I needed them today," he said. "Can you e-mail them to me?"

"I . . . uh," I started, but I knew it was time to come clean—at least about that. "Look, Alex, I lied about leaving them in the car today," I said in a low voice, turning my back on my mother. She was over by the open microwave, jabbing a fork into something that sounded frozen. I carried the cordless into the living room.

"You lied?" More silence. Then he said, "Why'd you lie?"

"Because I didn't think you'd understand. I didn't have time to get to them because I was so overwhelmed by studying and family stuff and . . ." *And kissing another guy,* I thought.

"Look, Jessica, I know you're busy. That's why I asked you if you were sure you could handle being features editor with everything else you've got going on. If you can't handle it—"

"I can handle it," I cut in. I felt awful for letting him down. "Really."

"I'm not sure about that," he answered.

"What are you saying?" I challenged him. "Do you want to kick me off yearbook? You can't! I worked really hard for this position, Alex!"

"Okay, calm down," he told me. "It's my job, as editor-in-chief, to stay on top of this stuff."

"Fine," I said. "I'll write up my ideas tonight, and give them to you tomorrow morning. "

"Don't hand in just anything, okay?" Alex warned me. "I want this to be really great."

"I'm not going to hand in just anything," I snapped. "I have some really good ideas. I just didn't have a chance to put them down on paper yet, okay?"

"Well . . . maybe I can get us another day," Alex suggested. "You and I can get together tomorrow night and brainstorm together."

Most other times, I would have been happy to do something like this with Alex. We always had fun bouncing ideas off each other. But tonight, his suggestion made it sound as if he didn't trust me to get the job done on my own. As if I needed his help to have creative and interesting ideas.

I was about to tell him off, when I stopped. What am I doing? I asked myself. *Why am I so angry at Alex? He's just trying to help me out.*

I knew the reason. I knew it was because I was feeling guilty about the horrible thing I'd done behind his back. Alex was my boyfriend, and I'd cheated on him. Not only that, I had agreed to see Scott again tomorrow. How could I explain that to Alex? I couldn't. *I shouldn't.*

"Okay," I said reluctantly. "I just have to cancel a meeting with my, uh, study partner. I was supposed to meet her at the library tomorrow night to go over some sociology notes." I made sure that I said "her" so he wouldn't get suspicious.

"Study partner? But I thought you just had a test in sociology today," he said.

"Uh . . . I did. But this is for midterms," I told Alex. "They're coming up really soon." I cleared my throat. "Well, see you tomorrow at school. Bye!" I quickly hung up.

I couldn't believe how easily one lie led to the next. *I'm digging a hole right under my feet,* I thought, *and slowly sinking in.*

"Hey, you look like yourself again," Alex said when we bumped into each other in the hallway at school the next morning.

"Yeah, I'm back." I tried to toss it off lightly, but it didn't quite come out that way. I was dressed in my usual wardrobe again—boring jeans and an even more boring blue crewneck sweater.

I'd been too tired to fuss about *the look* this morning. I'd stayed up really late last night working on my English paper. I was comparing the imagery of death and rebirth in two poems by Dickinson.

I'd been working so hard, it was really late before I noticed that Scott had never called me about tonight, like he said he would. I checked my e-mail once at night, hoping to see a message from him, but I found only a quick note from Kerri.

That had reminded me to send Maya a message, asking if she wanted to talk. But she never replied, so I figured she'd been out later than she'd expected with her father.

Whatever, I thought. *I'll cancel with Scott if I see him on campus later.*

Alex fell into step beside me as I headed down

the hall to my first class. He slung his arm around my shoulders and gave me an affectionate squeeze. "The other look was . . . interesting," Alex said. "But I like the familiar Jessica better."

I smiled, wrapping my arm around his waist. "I like the familiar too." It felt good to be walking through school like this with Alex again. I thought about what I had told my friends at Amber's house. That Alex was too nice.

Nice. That wasn't such a bad way to be, right? It was good, actually. And Alex was such a great guy. He wasn't even holding a grudge about the way I'd lied about those yearbook ideas. "So we're still getting together tonight, right?" I asked.

"Yeah, definitely," Alex replied. "Only not at my place."

"Okay, you can come to mine. But why?" We reached my homeroom and stopped walking.

"Things are kind of bad at home right now," he said with a shrug. "David and Betsy are arguing every second, and my parents are totally stressing about how small our house seems lately." Alex paused and shook his head. "Poor Josh. I think he's really feeling it. I'm trying to spend more time with him. You know, give him a little more attention. But it's really hard."

"Wow, sounds awful," I said.

He nodded. "It is. Sorry to dump this all on you, but sometimes you just need to tell someone."

"Hey, that's what I'm here for," I said, reaching out to ruffle his hair. I was glad that he could still open up to me.

Alex grinned at me. "Hey, I had this idea last night for a yearbook article—tell me what you think. After they announce the homecoming queen, we get a photographer to, like, follow her around and take all these candid shots. . . ."

Homecoming? I hadn't given homecoming a second thought since Sunday afternoon's meeting. But I had to start thinking about it. The nominations were being announced on Monday. Since I came in second last year, I was almost sure to get one. I had to plan my essay. I wasn't going to lose by three votes again. Yearbook wasn't the only thing I was letting slip, I realized.

"Hey, Jess," Alex said, breaking my thoughts. "Maybe I'll call a staff meeting for Saturday night at the Cellar or something. We can finalize the article ideas and then hang out. Sound good?"

"Sounds great," I said.

As I gazed up at Alex, I thought about how good-hearted and sweet he really was. I couldn't believe I'd even thought about going with another guy. I was determined to shift my attention back to where it belonged—which was right here, in South Central, with my boyfriend. My *real* boyfriend.

After English Lit that afternoon, I hung around the student union, sipping a Snapple and hoping I'd run into Scott so I could cancel our plans. I'd really enjoyed class today. Our professor talked a lot about one of the poems I'd picked for my paper, so I got some more good information. Her talk also made me feel on track with most of my ideas.

But as I sat there, halfheartedly taking more notes for the paper, I started to feel a little weird. What if Scott saw me here, and thought that I still wanted to go out with him? What if he wanted to kiss me again? Would I be able to say no?

I took a sip of my Snapple. *What am I getting so worried about?* I scolded myself. *He didn't even call me. He probably forgot about our plans anyway.*

Whatever, I thought, and decided to try to create something for my creative writing group. After all, we were meeting on Monday, and it would be nice if I had something to read to everybody.

I opened my backpack, and fished out the black-and-white composition book I used to write short stories in. I turned to a page, and stared at the tiny poem I had been working on.

I leave the life I love
To join the life I don't know
What am I afraid of?

Note to self, I thought. *Learn to accept your limitations.* Maybe poetry wasn't such a good idea. And maybe I should try to be creative at home.

I was just about to pack up my books, when I heard a familiar voice.

"Hey, Jessica!" Bree cried. She waved and walked over to me.

"Hi!" I said, thrilled to see a friendly face. "Want to sit down?"

"Sure, I have a few minutes to kill." Bree slid into the seat across from me. She made a little small talk about the sociology test, then said, "So how's it going with Scott? You two are getting together tonight, right?"

I hesitated. "We were supposed to, but . . ." I was too embarrassed to tell her he hadn't called. Instead, I said, "I've got to cancel. Something else came up."

"You're canceling a date with Scott Seifert?"

"How'd you know his last name?" I knew I hadn't mentioned it when I'd introduced them.

"Everybody knows Scott Seifert," Bree said. "He's hot." Then I saw this funny look on her face. "Oh, wow. Here he comes. I hope he didn't hear me," she muttered under her breath.

I turned to see Scott strolling across the union, wearing jeans and a beat-up green military-style jacket. He saw us and waved.

"Sorry I didn't call you last night, Jess," he said as he pulled a chair up to our table.

"No problem." I could feel Bree watching us really intensely. It made me feel sort of self-conscious. "I actually wasn't home anyway."

"Yeah, me neither. I went out to this party and I got home late. I didn't think Michelle and Frank would appreciate a four A.M. phone call from me."

"Who are Michelle and Frank?" Bree cut in.

"Her parents," Scott said.

I could tell Bree was impressed that he knew their names. I guess she figured we were really tight.

"Listen, Scott," I said. "I can't make it tonight after all." There. I'd gotten it out.

"You can't? That's too bad. I was looking forward to it."

"You were?" So that meant he had still planned for us to go out. *Well, that doesn't matter,* I reminded myself. *I can't go. I mean, I don't want to go. I'm meeting Alex. My boyfriend.*

"No big deal," he said quickly. Maybe a little too quickly, I thought. "We can do it some other time."

That was my cue to tell him I wouldn't be going

out with him again. Ever. But I didn't. I was too busy wondering why, if he had planned on keeping the date, he didn't seem more upset that I'd broken it.

"Hey, are you guys going to the party on the West Side Saturday night?" Bree asked.

"The one those guys Jeff and Blake are throwing?" Scott asked.

"Yeah. It's going to be killer," Bree said. "Jeff's brother works at a brewery in Milwaukee, and they're getting the beer for free. No cup charge."

"Cool. I'll be there." Scott looked at me. "You going, Jess?"

I perked up a little. "Definitely," I said.

I'd never been to a college party. For one thing, no one had ever told me about any. For another, I had my curfew, and I figured these things didn't even get under way till close to midnight. But curfew or not, I was determined to go to this one. Then maybe I'd feel as though I really fit in here. At the same time, though, I was a little disappointed that Scott hadn't asked me to go to the party *with* him—not that I wanted to go with him or anything.

"Well, I've gotta grab some caffeine and get to class. Bye, Bree," Scott said, swinging his backpack over his shoulder. He stared into my eyes for a second, and I felt my pulse go into overdrive. I couldn't help it. "See you later, Jess," he said.

"What a hottie," Bree breathed, watching him walk away. She was practically drooling. "You're really lucky he's so into you."

"You think he is?" I asked.

"Definitely."

I hesitated. "Don't you get the impression that he doesn't care that I broke our date?"

"That was a total act," she said. "The way he looks at you, Jess, he's totally into it."

Hearing Bree say that made me feel great. I mean, I didn't know her very well. She had no reason to say that just to make me feel better. It must really be true. *I hope Scott's not too upset when he finds out we're never going out again,* I thought.

Who was I kidding? I was still crazy about Scott. Now all I could think about was how dumb I'd been to cancel our date. I had this crazy impulse to catch up with him, and tell him I could see him tonight after all. But I wouldn't. I had to think of Alex.

"So why'd you break the date, anyway?" Bree asked.

"Oh, I've got to get together with someone about something for school," I said vaguely. Then I decided to be straight with her. "Actually, I'm seeing my boyfriend tonight. He goes to my school."

Bree giggled. "You know, I kind of forgot you were in high school."

"You did?" I grinned, totally flattered. But then I remembered something awful. "Oh, no! I can't go to the party on Saturday. I've got a yearbook meeting!"

"Just don't go," Bree said. "You can't miss this party."

"Yeah, but I can't miss the meeting either. I'm one of the editors. We have to finalize the articles."

"Really? Well that sounds . . . urgent." I saw Bree trying to hide a smirk.

Now I was embarrassed. The yearbook was a big deal in high school, especially senior year. But once you were in college, I guess it must seem pretty lame. Bree obviously thought so.

"Actually, I'm not really into it this year," I told her quickly. "I took the job last term, but I haven't done a thing so far. I wish I could just bag it, but I don't want to let everyone down."

"I'd blow it off anyway," Bree said. "I mean, which would you rather do? Finalize yearbook articles or party? Come on, Jess. It's a no-brainer."

"You're right," I told her. "I'm going to the party." After I finished, I couldn't quite believe what I had said. Did I really want to skip the meeting—after I practically had to beg Alex to keep me on staff?

"And while you're at it," Bree continued, "you should probably dump your high school boyfriend."

"You really think so?" I asked weakly.

"Give me a break." Bree looked as though she was beginning to lose her patience. "We're talking about Scott Seifert. He's totally hot for you."

"I guess," I said, almost wishing that he didn't even like me. My life would be so much easier.

Chapter 10

Late Saturday afternoon, Alex and I sat on the couch in my living room going over our list of feature ideas. We had put together about ten good ones the other night, even though we needed only five. The staff would discuss them at the meeting tonight and narrow down the list. I knew he wanted to be well prepared for the meeting, but he was overdoing it a little, I thought.

I pretended to listen to him go on and on about yearbook, but all I could think about was the party I had to miss.

I'd told Bree I was going to skip the yearbook meeting, but I'd realized there was no way I could get out of it. I really didn't want to lie to Alex again. Besides, my parents were having people over to play cards tonight, so there was no way around my curfew.

"And I thought if we did that feature about

teachers, we could ask them for their baby pictures and have sort of a match-up quiz with answers on another page," Alex was saying. "What do you think?"

"Sounds great," I told him. He added "teacher baby photos" to the list he was writing in a notebook.

My mother poked her head into the living room. "Dad and I are going out to pick up the bratwurst for tonight," she told me. "Should we get some extras for you two?"

"No, thanks," I said. "We're going to the Cellar later. We'll get something there."

"Oh, right. Your meeting." She waved. "Be back in a while."

I heard my parents go out the back door, and a minute later, their car pulled out of the driveway. I looked at Alex. "Alone at last," I said teasingly. But I actually meant it. We hadn't spent any time alone together all week.

"Your brother?" Alex asked.

"Packers game," I replied.

"Then come here," he said with a cute smile. I sat beside him, and we looked at each another a moment. Then he pulled me closer and gave me a sweet, lingering kiss.

I kissed him back, glad to know that Alex was still attracted to me—that it wasn't one-sided after all. Now I realized that maybe there was hope for us—that maybe seeing Scott was a big mistake. I mean, I loved Alex, and he loved me. We had an awesome relationship, and I'd nearly wrecked everything.

It felt so good to be in his arms like this. I slipped my hand under his sweater and stroked the bare skin on his stomach and chest. Alex kissed me deeper, and let out a little moan.

I slid my fingertips under the waistband of his jeans.

"Jess . . . we have to stop," he said, catching my hand. He sat up, moving away from me.

I flopped my head back against the arm of the couch, exasperated—and totally mortified.

"Look, we can't," Alex said. "Your parents—"

"Are gone," I reminded him, reeling with embarrassment. I felt like such a loser, being rejected like this. "They won't be back for at least an hour."

"Well, they're not the only reason we can't," Alex said, raking a hand through his hair. It fell neatly back into place.

I thought about Scott's unruly locks, about how he wouldn't have stopped if we were alone together. In fact, unlike Alex, Scott couldn't keep his hands off me. Then I thought about how I could have seen Scott tonight, at that party.

"Jess, come on. We've talked about this," Alex

reminded me. "We're not ready."

No, you're *not ready,* I corrected him mentally. But all I said aloud was, "You're right. I guess I got carried away."

"It happens," he said with a shrug and a smile.

Not to you, I thought. *How come it never happens to you?*

The homecoming queen nominations were announced during homeroom on Monday, with all the usual candidates—Lenore Rivera, Heather Thompson, Gretchen Jenkins . . .

When I heard my name, I was instantly psyched. But then I wondered what Bree and Scott would think, and some of the thrill went out of it.

When I heard Erin's name on the homecoming queen list, I was totally shocked. She wasn't even interested in running. Actually, she didn't even really like football. The only reason she went to the games was to hang out with me, Maya, and Kerri.

The bell rang, and I sped into the hallway, intent on finding Erin before her first class. I spotted her near her locker, looking a little dazed.

"No way," she said when I came closer. "There's no way I'm doing this."

"Come on, Erin," I told her. "What have you got to lose?"

Erin leaned against the row of lockers. "Come on, Jess. I'm not exactly the homecoming type," she said, slinging on her Powerpuff Girls backpack over her 1940s vintage dress. "And I'm not changing my style."

A couple of students and teachers called congratulations to us as we headed to our classes.

"Hey, guys," Kerri said, popping up behind us. She walked between us, and placed one hand on Erin's shoulder and the other on mine. "So how am I going to decide who to vote for, now that you're both running?"

"Erin's not doing it," I told her.

"She'd never win anyway," Heather Thompson said as she and two other girls passed us. "Just look at her."

"You wish you had as much style as I do, Heather!" Erin called after her. Then she turned back to Kerri and me, obviously irritated. "You know," she said, "maybe it's time to shake things up for homecoming. Maybe it's time someone like me won the crown!" Erin struck a regal pose. Then she laughed. "I'm doing it. Just to annoy Heather!"

"You go, Queen E!" Kerri jumped up and down. "Oh, wait. That still doesn't help me. Who am I going to vote for?"

"Vote for Heather," I said with a laugh.

"Oh, come on, Jessica," Kerri said. "Don't you want me to vote for you? Aren't you going to campaign?"

"I *think* I could squeeze campaigning for homecoming queen into my busy schedule," I joked.

"Tell me about it," Kerri said. "You've been late for after-school chorus all week, Jess, and you never eat lunch with us. You never just hang out anymore. Are you sure you have time for homecoming? I mean, it's obvious that you're beyond all this high school stuff."

Whoa, I thought. *Kerri's not kidding. Where is all this coming from?*

"Kerri!" Erin said. "Stop ragging on Jessica. Can't you see that she's really busy?"

"Yeah, but not too busy to run for homecoming queen," I said for Kerri's benefit. But inside I couldn't help thinking about how lame Bree thought yearbook was. She'd probably think homecoming was even lamer.

I was surprised to see Scott waiting for me outside my sociology class when I got to campus. "What are you doing here?" I asked him, trying to sound casual.

Scott unwrapped a stick of Big Red, and shoved it in his mouth. "Waiting for you," he said, crumpling the wrapper in his fist. "Where've you been?"

"Around," I told him, feeling a little thrill that he'd obviously missed me.

"Yeah? You weren't around Saturday night. I thought you'd be at that party."

"Something else came up," I said with a shrug. "How was it?"

"It was okay. Listen, there's another party I'm going to this weekend. Friday night. You busy?"

I hesitated. Friday was another home game at school.

"What, you have plans?" he asked, rolling the foil wrapper into a ball. "With your *boyfriend?*"

"There's a football game," I told him.

"So?" Scott said, making a face. "Does your *boyfriend* play on the team?"

"No," I said, wondering if he could possibly be jealous.

"How serious are you with him?" he asked after a minute, like it wasn't just out of the blue—like we were embroiled in this big discussion about my relationship with Alex.

I was so stunned I didn't know what to say.

"Not all that serious, I think." Scott stood so close that I could smell the cinnamon gum on his breath. "So you want to come to that party with me?"

With him? I'd thought he was just going to ask

me if I'd be there. A rush of excitement ran through my body. This—this was a date. He was definitely asking me out.

I heard myself say yes.

"Cool," he said, grinning. Then he leaned over and kissed me. It was a quick kiss, but not like a little peck. More like . . . well, more like something I wanted more of.

Chapter 11

I practically ran down State Street for my next class that afternoon. It seemed as if I was constantly late for my college classes these days.

Afterward, I stopped at the college library to check my e-mail. There was only one message there, from Kerri. It was the same e-mail, sent to Erin and me.

Hi, Guys, I got Maya to agree to come down to Bernie's Bagels. I have to work there tonight, starting at five, but we can meet before my shift. She really needs us right now and I want her to feel like we're there for her.

It was already after 4:30. Snatching up my books, I bolted from the library, and ran across campus to my mom's car. I drove to the bagel place as fast as I could without being ticketed.

I burst into Bernie's Bagels, which was crowded, and spotted my friends at a table in the corner.

"Hey, guys," I said, pulling over a chair and plopping myself down. They were already eating bagels. "How's it going?"

"Okay. Aren't you going to order anything?" Erin asked, taking a sip of her cappuccino.

"Nah. I'm broke."

"I'll treat you," Maya offered, reaching into her pocket.

"It's okay. I'm not hungry anyway," I told her.

"Look, there's Luke Perez," Kerri said, waving. He'd just walked in the door alone. He saw us and came over.

"Hey," he said, kind of ducking his head in that shy way he had. "What's up?"

We all said, "Nothing," except Maya, who literally said nothing.

"How's it going, Maya?" Luke asked her.

"Okay," she said, not looking at him. She stared at her blueberry bagel as though it was the most fascinating thing she'd ever seen.

"You going to the game on Friday night?" Luke asked.

"No," she said. That was it. Just no.

Luke shrugged, then walked away, mumbling, "See ya."

"What's wrong with you, Maya?" Kerri asked.

"You always go to the games," Erin said. "Why'd you say no?"

"He obviously likes you," I pointed out. "And I think he's really nice." I remembered how he'd stuck up for Maya when T.J.'s stupid friends were mouthing off about her.

"So? I just don't feel like going, okay?" Maya scowled.

There was a long moment of silence at our table, except for the jazz blasting over the speakers.

I knew the whole thing with T.J. was still bothering her, but she never wanted to talk about it.

Then Kerri said, "Listen, Maya. You can't let this thing with T.J. get to you so bad. You have to stop blaming yourself. Remember what we talked about on Sunday?"

"Kerri's right," Erin added. "You seemed really resolved about it. What happened?"

Maya shrugged, still staring down at her bagel. "It has nothing to do with T.J. Miller. I just don't want to go to the game on Friday, so let's just drop it, okay?"

Erin and Kerri glanced at each other. Meanwhile, my thoughts were spinning, and I was feeling totally left out.

My friends had obviously gotten together to help

Maya without me. I'd gone to the college library to study, but I would have skipped the library to see them, especially for something this important. But they hadn't even called. I felt horribly hurt. Almost too hurt to say anything.

But Kerri must have noticed the look on my face. "Erin and I got together on Sunday afternoon and hung out with Maya. We didn't plan it or anything, but we just got talking about this T.J. thing."

"We called your house, Jess," Erin said. "But your mom said you were at the library."

"Oh, yeah. I was studying," I said. Now I remembered that my mother had mentioned that Erin called. But I'd never bothered to call her back. I figured I'd catch her in school the next day.

The fact that they'd called made me feel a little better, I guess.

Kerri cleared her throat. "Listen, guys. I was thinking we could go out after the game Friday night. You could meet us then, Maya," she added.

"Hey, Mr. Calvert told me about this really cool club he goes to," Erin said. "It has three floors of different kinds of music. Friday is sixteen-and-over night."

"Mr. Calvert goes club-hopping?" I asked. That was so strange. I couldn't picture him out partying.

"He's only twenty-six," Erin said. "So Friday

night sounds great. How about you, Maya? Jess?"

"There's this college party that night," I said reluctantly. "I'm going with Scott."

"Scott?" all three of them echoed.

"What about Alex?" Maya asked.

"What about football?" Kerri added. "Aren't you even coming to the game?"

I wanted to ask her what would be the big deal if I missed one. I mean, what was up with this town and football games? "I can go to the game first, and the party later," I told Kerri, realizing I'd better not alienate my friends.

"You know, Jess," Kerri said, staring at me, "it seems like your heart isn't in it."

"What's that supposed to mean? I said I was going."

"Yeah, but you don't look thrilled. Just like you weren't thrilled to get the homecoming queen nomination. And you don't seem thrilled to be hanging out with us lately, either."

Guilt washed over me as I looked from Kerri to Maya to Erin. I guessed she was right, in a way.

"Why don't you guys come to the college party with us?" I heard myself ask. They definitely looked interested. Even Maya seemed to perk up.

"But you can't say anything about this to anyone," I added quickly, before they could reply. "If it gets back to Alex, I'm dead."

"Well, what's up with you two anyway?" Erin asked.

"Yeah, are you and Scott together now?" Kerri asked. "Are you going to dump Alex for him?"

I wanted to say no, of course not. But I couldn't lie. "I don't know," I admitted. "I'm totally confused. I really like Scott, but Alex and I are . . . well, Alex is a huge part of my life."

"Just go with the flow, Jess," Erin advised.

"Yeah, that's fine for now," Maya pointed out. "But sooner or later she's going to have to make up her mind."

"I know," I said. "I'm *so* not looking forward to that."

"Well, you don't have to do it now. Wait till after homecoming," Kerri said. "Alex is your escort, right?"

"Of course." I frowned. I couldn't imagine Scott doing something like that.

"Who's going to go with you, Erin?" Maya asked.

"Yeah, too bad Keith doesn't live here," I said.

"How about Mr. Calvert?" Kerri cracked.

We all laughed . . . except for Erin, who turned bright red. "We're just friends, you guys."

"No kidding," I said. "Kerri was just teasing."

"Yeah, he's a teacher, Erin," Maya said. "What else would you be?"

Erin squirmed and looked embarrassed. I had to change the subject to get her off the hook, so I blurted out, "Hey, how about Glen? He could take you."

"Yeah, Glen." Erin nodded. "I thought of that too. I guess I was just wishing Keith could be here. I keep trying to think of a way to get him here, but it's impossible. I might as well ask Glen."

"He'll do," Kerri said. "He's cute and everything. You can send Keith a picture and make him jealous."

"I don't need to make Keith jealous. Things are great. Really great."

If you asked me, she sounded like she was trying to convince herself as well as us. I didn't know how two people could really keep such a long-distance romance going, but I didn't say anything.

"Hey, Jess," Erin said after a minute. "Want to get together and work on our homecoming essays tomorrow afternoon after school?"

"I can't. I'm meeting my creative writing group at the Empty Cup Café."

"How's that going?" Maya asked.

"Okay, I guess," I replied, "but it's hard to find time to be creative when you're stressed with schoolwork."

"How about if I meet you at the Empty Cup after your group is finished," Erin suggested. "We can work on our essays then."

"Why not?" I told her.

"I'll pop by too, when I get out of work," Kerri said. "A lot of college kids hang out there. Maybe we'll meet some friends of yours so we'll know someone Friday night."

I sat silently as my frinds started talking about how much fun the party was going to be. Erin knew the exact outfit she was going to wear, and Maya wondered whether she should drink beer or mixed drinks, and how she was going to get out of her curfew. They kept going on and on.

And all I could think about was how they were acting pretty immature. I mean, I loved them, but maybe it wasn't such a good idea to bring them to this party after all. High school and college were completely different worlds, and now I wasn't so sure anymore if I should mix them.

Oh, well, I thought. *Too late now.* But I had the feeling that something awful was going to happen on Friday night, and there was no way I could stop it.

Chapter 12

The Empty Cup Café was totally jammed with people. I sat on a velvet couch in the corner of the dimly-lit coffee house with the other members of my writing group.

I shifted my weight back and forth uncomfortably as a guy named Trey, who had dreadlocks and five-o'clock shadow, read a long poem about racism.

I thought back to the story I had read earlier—about a rose that overcame its fear of thunder. It was supposed to be a metaphor for the relationships kids have with their parents, and I had thought it was pretty good, but now I was beginning to wonder if I even had talent.

Compared to Trey's, my work seemed so simple and trite. I knew that I needed to spend more time on my writing if I ever wanted to be good. I just didn't know when that would actually happen.

I could see Erin and Kerri at a round table over

by the door. They were sitting with Alex, who had brought Josh. I kept wondering what they were doing here.

Josh kept waving at me, which would have been kind of embarrassing except that he was so incredibly sweet. His nose was running from the cold he'd had all week. Alex took a tissue from his pocket and gently wiped Josh's nose.

He was so tender with Josh, and I knew that he was going to be a great dad someday. I got this weird hollow feeling inside at the thought.

Finally, my writing group meeting was finished, and I crossed the room to where my friends were sitting.

"Hey, guys," I said, ruffling Josh's hair. "What are you two doing here?" I asked Alex.

"We ran into Erin down the street, and she said she was meeting you, so we thought we'd say hi," Alex said. "Josh and I just went to see the new Disney movie."

"It was so cool, Jessic," Josh exclaimed. "There was this huge monster who—"

"Keep it down, Josh," Alex cautioned him. I noticed that a bunch of college kids at the next table were looking over at us, as if they were wondering what this little kid was doing here.

I was kind of glad when Alex took Josh to the

men's room to wipe his nose. Not that I was embarrassed to be seen with them or anything, but . . . well, I didn't like sticking out in a crowd, and with Josh, we definitely stood out.

"Hey, Jessica," a guy said as he passed our table.

I vaguely recognized him from my English Literature class. "Hi," I said, surprised he even knew my name. I mean, he was really cute—not the kind of guy you'd think would pay attention to remembering someone like me. He was with a friend, also really cute.

Kerri kicked me under the table. "Introduce us, Jess," she whispered.

I wanted to strangle her. I couldn't remember the first guy's name, and I had never seen his friend before in my life. Now the two of them had kind of parked themselves by our table.

"Hey, did you hand in your paper?" asked the first guy.

"Sure," I said. "It was due last week." Then I jumped a little as Kerri kicked me again.

"I didn't even start it yet. Hey, are you okay?" the guy asked.

"She's fine," Kerri said. "I'm Kerri. This is Erin. We're friends of Jessica's."

"I'm gonna get another coffee," I said, standing. I didn't really want another cup, but I suddenly needed to get away from my friends for a few minutes.

I went to the counter, placed my order, then stepped aside to wait for it. I was only a few feet away from the table where my friends were sitting, and I could hear them talking to the guys.

"I've never seen you around before," one of them said, checking Kerri out like he totally appreciated what he saw. "Which dorm do you live in?"

"We don't live on campus," Erin said. "So do you guys have names, or what?"

I sighed inwardly, knowing that they'd never get away with passing themselves off as college students. Not that I was so sophisticated, but at least I was taking classes at the university. They didn't even know any of the professors.

"I'm Brent, and this is Chris. Where off campus?" the guy asked.

"Kensington Heights," Erin replied.

"Where's that?" Chris asked.

Maya, Erin, and Kerri glanced at one another. I think they realized Erin had almost blown it for them. If they didn't think of something fast, the guys would probably catch on that they were still in high school.

The counter guy handed me my coffee, but I just stood there, holding it, not wanting to go back to the table.

"Hey, wait, I know where it is," Brent said. "There's no campus housing there. It's, like, families and stuff."

"Right. We kind of live at home," Erin admitted reluctantly.

"We commute," Kerri tried to cover.

"What parking lot do you use?" Chris asked. It was obvious to me that he was suspicious.

"The, uh . . . regular one," Erin bluffed.

Brent and Chris exchanged knowing looks. "You girls aren't in college, are you?"

"We will be, in less than a year," Kerri replied.

Chris checked his watch. "Better drink up. You must be getting close to your curfew." He and Brent cracked up.

I felt like jumping in, defending my friends and telling these two losers what jerks they were. But for some reason, I couldn't say anything. Actually, for a specific reason. Brent and Chris didn't know how old I was. If I said something then they would know I was one of them—one of these high school girls they found so amusing. What if they were at the party on Friday night? They might make fun of me. I'd be totally humiliated.

"Oh, that's really mature of you," Erin was saying. "You guys might be in college, but you're acting like you're in pre-K."

"Yeah, in, like, ten months we'll be in college, too," Kerri said. "It's not that big a deal."

The guys walked away, elbowing each other in the ribs like they thought the whole thing was hilarious.

Erin's gaze fell on me. Kerri noticed too.

"God, Jess, why are you just standing there?" Kerri asked.

"Didn't you hear what those jerks were saying?" Erin added.

"Of course she heard, Erin," Kerri said. "That's why she didn't come back. She didn't want them to know she was with us."

"That's not true," I said, but my voice shook, and I knew that they knew I was lying. It *was* true, and I felt really awful about it.

"You know, they're probably just a couple of dumb frat boys," Erin said as I sat down. "Who cares what they think?"

I cared. But I couldn't admit it.

"I hope there are nicer guys than those two at the party," Kerri commented.

The party. I saw now that the party was going to be a total disaster. They just wouldn't fit in. They were still way too high school.

I was glad to see Alex and Josh coming back to the table. I slid over to make room for them, and changed the subject to homecoming. Then Kerri talked about Friday night's football game.

"Maybe we'll actually make it to Pizza Pi before the game this time," Alex told me.

"Yay!" Josh cried. "I love pizza."

Erin was unusually quiet. She looked as though she was deep in thought. Was she thinking about Keith?

"You guys, I can't figure out what to tell my parents about the party," she burst out.

I froze, stunned. *No, she didn't just say that,* I thought.

"What party?" Alex asked me.

"Uh, well there was this college party these guys wanted to go to," I said quickly. "But it was canceled."

My friends looked surprised. Then Kerri gave me a wink behind Alex's back, to show she knew I was just saying that for Alex's benefit.

"Were you going too?" he asked. There was something irritating about his expression.

"I was thinking about it," I said. But actually I was thinking that there was no reason I had to feel so guilty for going to a party without him.

Okay, so there was a reason. Scott. But Alex didn't know about that part. He was all mad, just because I was thinking about going to a college party, period. Like he owned me or something.

"You were?" Alex asked. Now he wasn't so much mad as he was hurt.

"It wouldn't start until after the game is over," I said with a pang of guilt, "and I knew you'd have to get Josh home."

"Yeah, which is what I have to do right now," he said, shoving back his chair and standing abruptly. "Come on, Josh. We were supposed to be home a half hour ago."

Josh protested, and Alex was short with him, which wasn't like him. I looked at my friends as Alex and Josh walked away.

"Erin!" Maya stared at her. "I can't believe you did that! I mean, I don't know what I'm going to tell my dad either, but I didn't say anything."

Erin sunk in her chair. "I'm so sorry, Jess," she said. "It just slipped out."

"Don't worry, Jessica," Kerri said. "Alex will never know that we all went to the party. We won't say a word." She looked across the table. "Right, Erin?"

"No," I cut in. "It really is canceled. I just found out today, and I was going to tell you guys as soon as I had the chance, but Alex was here, so . . ."

"You're kidding." Kerri frowned. "And I was really looking forward to it."

"So was I," Erin said.

Maya shrugged. "At least now we don't have to

try and come up with a way to stay out past curfew," she said.

I felt terrible for lying to my friends, but that wasn't the worst of it. If I still wanted to go to the party with Scott—and I did—I'd have to lie to them once again.

Chapter 13

Friday night, and my plan was totally under way. I'd left my parents a note that said I was staying over at Kerri's. I slept there all the time, so I knew they'd never call and check.

Mom and Dad weren't going to the game, so there was no chance they'd run into my friends and bring it up. They had to go to some retirement party for someone my dad worked with, which really upset them because it meant they'd have to miss seeing Ricky play.

Later I planned on telling Kerri, Maya, and Erin that I'd missed the football game because I got held up at the college library. Alex hadn't been in school today, and when I called him, he said he had a nasty cold and wouldn't be going to the game.

The whole thing couldn't have worked out more perfectly for me. I told Scott that I'd meet him at the party, and Bree said I could go with her and some of her friends. She said I could crash at her dorm afterward if I wanted, so I'd packed some stuff to take with me.

I drove over to the university, and parked in the regular commuter lot. I'd never been on campus this late on a Friday night, and I noticed that the atmosphere was different. Now there was this kind of festive electricity, and everywhere I looked, there were groups of people on their way back from the dining halls or just hanging out in front of the dorms. I felt kind of conspicuous walking around with my old flowered overnight bag—like a little kid going off to spend the night at Grandma's house, or something.

In the lobby of Bree's dorm, I sat down, looking around. I'd never been inside a dorm before and felt a little weird sitting there by myself. There were posters up on every wall, announcing sports events and dorm activities or whatever.

A few kids wandered through the lobby and stopped to chat with one another. Everyone was so casual, and seemed to belong, and I wondered how many people were freshmen. It was impossible to tell. I mean, no one looked lost or lonely . . . except me.

I couldn't help wondering what I was even doing there. I mean, who was I trying to kid?

"Jessica!" Bree called, stepping through the

front door. "You're here. Great!"

"Hi!" Her very presence made me immediately feel better.

"This is Micah, my roommate," she said, introducing me to the girl with her.

Micah was a gorgeous African American, with long, spiral-curled hair and sparkly dark eyes. She gave me a big smile, and I liked her right away.

"You must be psyched about the party," she said.

"I am," I replied, trying not to sound too psyched. The three of us headed upstairs, with me lugging my bag.

"Come on inside," Bree said, opening a door. "We have to get you all set for your big date with the hottest hottie on campus."

The room they shared wasn't that big, but there was a pretty braided rug on the floor and chintz bedspreads and curtains and lots of plants and bowls of potpourri. They'd stored stuff like magazines and shoes and accessories in big baskets.

I looked around, deciding I wouldn't mind living like this—even though my room at home was twice as big and I didn't have to share it.

Micah immediately put on some hip-hop music, then flopped down on the bed closest to the window.

"You can stick your bag on my desk," Bree told me, pointing.

I did, and then I sat on the edge of the other bed, again feeling slightly self-conscious. It wasn't that Bree and Micah weren't being nice and friendly and welcoming, because they were. But I wasn't part of this, not really. And suddenly I wanted to be, more than anything.

Bree lit a cigarette and sat down next to me. "Want one?"

"Uh . . . I have some," I told her, debating whether or not to smoke. I still had that same pack of Marlboros in my jacket pocket, although they were probably all crushed by now. But maybe it'd help relax me. Maybe I'd feel like I fit in better. I started digging for the pack.

"Another smoker?" Micah reached over and opened the window.

"Oh, please, Mike." Bree laughed and offered me a light.

I hesitated. "Is it okay?"

"It's fine with me," Micah said. "I don't care if you both die of cancer. I just don't want all my clothes to smell smoky."

"So," Bree said, kicking off her chunky-heeled shoes. "Who wants a drink?"

Micah perked right up at that. "What do we have?"

Bree reached under her bed and produced a

bottle. "Vodka. The good kind."

"Let's see what we have for mixer," Micah said, opening the fridge. "Oh, this will work." She held up a bottle of Diet 7-Up. "What do you think?"

"Great," I said, like I knew what I was talking about.

Bree took out three blue plastic cups, lined them up on Micah's desk, and poured a major amount of vodka into each one.

Micah added soda, and then stirred each one with her finger.

Bree handed me a cup. "Cheers."

"Cheers," I said, and clinked cups with them both.

I took a sip. It was so strong it tasted kind of awful—kind of like how rubbing alcohol smelled. But then, after a few more swallows, I decided it wasn't really so bad.

Bree lit another cigarette from the one she'd smoked almost down to the filter, then bopped across the room to turn up the stereo. "I love Friday nights," she announced, dancing, her short hair flipping around on her head.

I wondered what it must be like to be so uninhibited. Bree didn't seem to spend a lot of time caring what people thought about her. I was the total opposite lately. Worrying about fitting in was practically my full-time occupation these days.

I was starting to feel a little buzzed from my drink and the cigarette, and I knew I was going to have to take it easy or I'd never make it to the party.

"Are you going to Wisconsin next year?" Micah asked me.

"Uh-uh. I want to go to NYU."

Micah shook her head. "Why would you want to go to college in a huge city? When I think of college, I think of a place like this. You know, old buildings and ivy-covered walls—"

"Yeah, it is great here," I admitted. I wondered what it would be like to stay next year. Maybe I wouldn't have to live at home. Maybe I could live in the dorms or get an apartment someplace near campus. . . .

Suddenly I didn't know how I felt about next year anymore. I vowed not to think about it tonight, though. Tonight was about my first college party—and having fun.

We could hear the music when we were still a block away from the party. I stuck close to Bree as the three of us walked up the steps, hoping no one could tell that I was just a little high school kid in disguise.

A shirtless guy was standing at the front door,

holding a stack of plastic cups and a black marker. "It's four bucks each for cups."

I handed him a ten-dollar bill.

He pulled an enormous wad of money out of his pocket. I looked over at Bree, surprised by all the cash.

"They have parties to make money for rent," she whispered.

I couldn't believe it. I wondered if there was anything illegal about doing something like that. Probably. But nobody else seemed fazed, so I acted cool as the guy counted out my change.

"Hand," the guy said.

"Huh?" I had no idea what he meant.

"Hold out your hand," he ordered impatiently, and I did. He turned it over and drew something with his black marker.

"Next," he barked, and Bree stepped forward.

I moved away and looked down to see what he drew. It looked like a W with two small dots at the bottom of the curves—oh, gross. It was a crude picture of a pair of boobs, the kind the boys used to draw in seventh grade. "What's this supposed to mean?" I asked Bree when he was done with her and had moved on to Micah's hand.

"It's kind of a stamp. You know, to show that you've paid." She examined her hand. "This is a little better than what they were drawing last week."

"I don't even want to know." I wrinkled my nose.

Inside, the party was wall-to-wall people. I looked around for Scott, but I didn't see him.

"Come on, let's get some beer," said Micah, as she and Bree pushed through the crowd.

We were standing at the foot of a battered staircase that must have been beautiful about a hundred years ago. Now it was all beat up. In some spots the faded wallpaper was peeled off in giant patches, and the floors were scuffed and sticky.

"The keg's probably in the kitchen again," Bree announced.

Beer sounded disgusting after all that vodka, and I had always heard that you weren't supposed to mix. Still, I followed the two of them down this long hall to a kitchen. There was a keg in a metal tub near the back door, surrounded by people holding empty cups and waiting for the tap. Finally Bree, Micah, and I worked our way to the front and filled our plastic cups with beer.

I didn't see any familiar faces, and actually, this whole scene was kind of intimidating. I mean, it wasn't like I was expecting balloons and Pin the Tail on the Donkey, but this . . .

Some girl jostled Bree's arm from behind on her way to the keg, and beer sloshed over the top of her cup. "It's getting too crowded in here," Bree said, wiping beer off her shirt. "Let's go into the other room." I followed her, and so did Micah.

I sipped my beer, looking around the dark and smoky room. Still no Scott.

Bree lit up a cigarette and so did I. It was something to do, I guessed. This party wasn't all that great. I found myself wishing Kerri, Maya, and Erin were here after all. Having them around wouldn't be so bad. Maybe nobody would have known they were only in high school.

I felt guilty for having lied to them. *What if they found out the party wasn't canceled? They'll never find out,* I told myself. *Stop worrying and have fun.*

The next hour zoomed by as the party became more and more crowded. Some guy came by a few times with a pitcher and refilled our cups. Bree and Micah introduced me to a lot of people, and we had brief, shouted conversations over the blaring music.

Everything was becoming a pleasant blur.

At some point the room turned into a dance floor, and before I knew it I was jamming with everyone else. I was starting to feel better about being here. Besides, I couldn't just stand there when everyone else was dancing.

Then all of a sudden he was there, in front of me. Scott just stood there, watching me dance. His arms were folded in front of him, and he was wearing this sexy grin. He looked so amazing that my heart started pounding like crazy.

We stared at each other, then he said, "Hi."

Boldly, I danced a few steps closer to him. "Hi."

"What time do you have to be home?" he asked.

I tossed my head a little, flirting with him. "I don't."

He raised his eyebrows. "Good." Then he lowered his eyes, blatantly checking me out from head to toe. "You look . . ." he trailed off and shook his head, grinning.

"So do you," I told him.

"C'mere," he said, and reached out. His hand closed over my upper arm, and the next thing I knew, he was pulling me up against him. His lips covered mine in a crushing kiss.

I forgot where we were. I forgot everything except this incredible sensation. We moved into a dark corner of the room and stood there, making out, for a long, long time.

We were both carried away, but I didn't want to stop.

I couldn't stop.

And then he led me away, our hands clasped as we pushed through the crowds to the stairway by the door. My head was spinning, and I couldn't even

definitely have left together. No matter what he said about being okay with my decision, he obviously wasn't.

"Okay," I said, and left him standing there.

I went to find my coat and ran into Bree and Micah. They had their arms around each other and were singing "Margaritaville" at the top of their lungs. They looked wrecked.

"Jessie!" Bree shouted, really dragging out the s's. "Where've you been? Where's Scott?"

"I have no idea," I told her, grabbing my coat off a chair. "Listen, I'm leaving. I'll see you on Monday. Bring my stuff to class, okay?"

"Okay," Bree chirped. "See ya." She waved drunkenly.

I made my way to the door, hoping I'd see Scott on my way out. I didn't, and I decided not to go back and find him to say good-bye. *Let him wonder about that,* I thought as I stepped into the chilly night.

I'd driven to campus, but decided it would be better for me not to drive home since I'd been drinking. I could take the bus home and come back for my car the next day. It was past midnight, but the stop was just down the block at the corner. A bus would probably come along soon.

I walked to the corner, which was pretty deserted, and I started to get the creeps. *Maybe I shouldn't have left the party,* I thought. *At least, not by myself. Maybe I could have talked Scott into coming with me.*

Then I wondered if I had been too hard on him. After all, I'd let things go pretty far, then at the last minute, I had said no. I couldn't really blame Scott for being kind of cold to me.

But then I figured he'd get over it. He was probably over it already. I thought about that for a few minutes, and decided I needed to talk to him. I turned around and started walking back to the party.

As soon as I stepped back into the house, I saw that things had really gotten out of hand since I'd left. Some girl was passed out on the floor inside the door, and I heard a guy puking his guts up somewhere. A bunch of people were having a loud argument by the keg in the kitchen.

I spotted Micah as I walked back toward the door. "Jessica!" she exclaimed. "I thought you'd left."

"I came back," I said. "Listen, have you seen Scott?"

I knew by the look on her face that something was up.

"He's with someone, isn't he," I said, feeling nauseous.

"Look, Jessica, it's not what you—"

I didn't bother listening to Micah any longer. I

took off up the stairs. Something told me I'd find him in the same room we'd been in before. But even as I went toward it, I thought I had to be wrong. He wouldn't be here with another girl so soon after I'd left.

The door was ajar, I saw with relief. Good. The room had to be empty. Then I heard a sound from inside.

It's probably somebody else, I told myself. Just because somebody was in there, it didn't mean that it was Scott. Maybe Micah was wrong.

Still, I had to know. I pushed the door open a few inches—and stared in absolute horror. The room was totally dark, but I could see a couple together on the bed.

Scott . . . and Bree.

Chapter 15

All I wanted to do was get into my bed and pull the covers over my head. I still couldn't believe what I'd seen back at the party. I kept telling myself it had to be some mistake, but inside I knew that it wasn't.

Bree and Scott, together. They'd been so busy with what they were doing that neither of them even noticed me. My stomach curdled just thinking about it.

"Jessica?" my mother called from the living room as I pushed the front door open. She clicked on the light.

I froze. She's awake? Uh-oh.

"Yeah?" I stepped into the hall, trying frantically to come up with an explanation. *I'll say that I felt sick at Kerri's, and decided to come home and sleep in my own bed, and I couldn't drive because . . .*

"Come in here, Jessica." I heard my father say, and he didn't sound happy.

They were sitting there next to each other on the powder blue couch with their arms folded.

· And they looked furious.

This was turning into my worst nightmare. My stomach churned. "What's up?" I asked, trying to sound casual.

"Where have you been?" my father shouted, and rose from the couch.

Oh, God, I thought. "What do you mean? Didn't you get my note? I was sleeping over at Kerri's." At this point, it was probably stupid to continue the lie, but what else could I do?

"You weren't at Kerri's, Jessica," my mother said. "We saw her."

"You saw her? Where?"

"At the game." My father stood and walked toward me.

"I—I thought you weren't going to the game," I stammered. "I thought you had some retirement dinner."

"We decided not to go," Mom said.

"You didn't tell me that!" I cried. Okay, so maybe I didn't have a right to be upset about that, since I did lie to them. But still . . .

"We saw Kerri right after the game," my mother said, "and she said she hadn't seen you all night. She said you were supposed to be there. When we told her you'd said you were sleeping over at her house, it was obvious she had no idea what we where talking about, even though she tried to make us think otherwise."

I swallowed hard. Good old Kerri. She'd tried to help, even though she'd been sort of angry with me lately.

"You lied to us, Jessica. And we deserve an explanation. Where have you been?" My father repeated through clenched teeth, obviously trying to stay in control.

"I was at a dorm on campus. My friend Bree, from college, asked me to spend the night with her so that we could work on a project we're doing for class," I said, sniffling.

They stared at me.

I stared back. Could they tell it wasn't the whole truth?

"Why didn't you ask us if you could go?" my mother asked evenly.

"Because I didn't think you'd let me. You always treat me like a little kid."

My father shook his head. "You act like one, sneaking around behind our backs and lying. I expect more from you."

My mother looked at me sadly. "We trusted you, Jessica."

I knew they were disappointed in me, and I hated hurting them. Anger, I could take. This, I couldn't. What would they think of me if they knew the rest of the story?

I couldn't handle any of this. Bree and Scott, my parents, my friends, Alex. . . . My whole world was upside down, and all I wanted was for things to go back to the way they were.

"You deserve to be grounded," my father said, "and believe me, I'm ready to do it."

"But, Dad, I didn't mean to do anything so wrong," I told him. "All I wanted was to spend some time on campus, with my new friends."

"You lied about who you were with," my mom reminded me.

"But I was studying," I protested, lying again. There seemed no way around it. I couldn't let them ground me. "You treat me like a baby. I'm in college now."

"You're in *high school*," my father said.

"But college, too. I've got new responsibilities. I need more freedom. How do you expect to talk me into staying home next year when you treat me like I'm in prison?"

My parents exchanged a glance. To my surprise, when my mother looked at me, it was almost as if she understood.

"I told Dad that grounding you was too harsh," she said. "You have a lot going on this year at school—and then there's homecoming," she added, catching me off guard. "You're nominated for queen, and it's a once in a lifetime thing."

I remembered how she'd told me she'd always wished she could run for homecoming queen, but she'd never been nominated. It was almost as if she wanted me to do it because she couldn't. Football, homecoming—traditions like that were such a huge deal to my parents.

"Your mom said it would be too awkward for you to bow out now if we grounded you," Dad said gruffly.

"Thanks," I murmured, but I guess it didn't really matter if I was grounded or not. I had lost Scott to Bree, a girl I'd thought was a friend. On top of that, I would probably end up losing Alex. And now I had some explaining to do to Kerri, Maya, and Erin. I'd lied to my best friends. Was I going to lose them too?

The first thing I did when I woke up the next morning was check my e-mail. Nothing—not even spam. I had been hoping my friends had written me, but what was I thinking? They were probably furious.

I went downstairs to call Kerri and saw that it

was actually almost noon. I'd been so exhausted I'd slept in, which I rarely did these days.

As I dialed Kerri's number I looked out the window at the gray, wet Saturday. My parents had left a note saying they'd taken Ricky to the mall to buy him new sneakers.

"Kerri?" I asked when she answered.

"No, this is Liz," her mom said. She always sounded just like Kerri on the phone. "Is this Jessica?"

"Yeah," I said, feeling guilty, as if even she knew what I'd been up to. Kerri's mom is so different from my mom—she's younger, for one thing, and she likes us to call her by her first name. She's into all this New Age stuff, like yoga and feng shui. Plus she's a guidance counselor, so she kind of understands how things work better than my mom, who is totally out of touch.

"How's it going?" Liz asked in this really casual way. So I guessed she didn't know. Then she called to Kerri.

A second later Kerri came on the line. "Hi," she said, her voice definitely sounding cold.

"Look, I'm sorry about last night, with my parents," I said right up front. "I told them I was sleeping over at your house."

"Yeah, no kidding. I felt like an idiot. I tried to

cover for you, but they didn't believe me."

"Thanks for trying."

"So where were you?" Kerri asked.

I cleared my throat. "I, uh, went to a party near campus."

Silence. Tense silence.

"I figured that much," she said finally. "It wasn't really canceled, was it?"

This whole story flashed through my head, about how the party I had told her about really had been canceled and that this was a different party—but then I reminded myself that I was telling the truth here. Funny how easily you can get so used to lying after a while.

"Why'd you tell us it was off?" Kerri asked.

"I wanted to be alone with Scott," I admitted, "without everyone tagging along," which was sort of the truth. There was no reason to tell her that I thought she, Maya, and Erin were too immature to be seen with.

Kerri sighed. "Then why didn't you just say that?"

"I don't know," I replied, feeling miserable. All I wanted was for her to forgive me, but I could tell things weren't going to get back to normal that easily.

"So how was it?" Kerri asked after another awkward silence.

"Actually, it was pretty awful," I told her.

"Really?" She sounded detached.

"Come on, Kerri," I said, swallowing what was left of my pride. "Please. Everything is so messed up and I don't know what to do. I need to talk to you." My voice cracked and I shut my mouth, not wanting to break down and cry.

"What's going on with you, Jess?" she asked, giving in.

Relieved, I started telling her. "The party was kind of dull at first. I mean Bree and Micah were having a good time, but I kept wishing that you guys were there. Anyway—"

"Wait," Kerri interrupted. "I thought you were going to the party with Scott. That's why you didn't want us around."

"But I didn't know I wasn't going with him until yesterday," I replied, cringing inside. After all, she was right.

"Still, you could've asked us to come when you found out. You obviously wanted to hang out with a bunch of college girls instead of being with us. How do you think that makes me feel?"

"Kerri, I'm so sorry about that. I shouldn't have lied to you guys," I told her. "I feel like a real jerk, but—"

"You are a jerk," Kerri cut in. "Look, I'd really

like to stay here and listen to your problems, but I've got to go—Erin's coming over. So . . ."

"She is?" I asked, feeling a little hurt. Erin and Kerri had made plans without me?

"Are you deaf now?" Kerri asked me. "Anyway, I have to take a shower. Bye, Jessica."

Click.

She hung up on me. I stood there a moment, just listening to the dial tone. *I'm losing my best friend,* I thought, stunned. *And it's all my fault.* I placed the phone back onto its cradle. I had to find a way to make Kerri listen so I could apologize, and promise to be a better friend. She deserved a better friend. Erin and Maya did too.

I didn't care that I had a ton of reading to do for English Lit or that I was supposed to come up with outlines for those yearbook features Alex and I had agreed on. My friendship with Kerri was more important. *I'm going over there,* I decided.

But first I had to call Alex. I picked up the phone again, and dialed his number.

He answered, but I almost didn't recognize him. His voice was totally hoarse from his cold. Instant guilt. I was out almost having sex with another guy while he was so sick.

"You sound terrible," I told him.

"I feel terrible. How was the game last night?"

"I ended up not going," I said, and before he could ask why not, I told him, "I have to go over to Kerri's later. Do you want me to bring you anything? Cough drops? Chicken soup?" I pulled some Cap'n Crunch from the cabinet and started munching on it, hoping to emphasize how casual this whole conversation was—that I wasn't trying to hide anything.

"That sounds sweet, but you should definitely stay away. I'm totally contagious. I'm sure I picked this up from Josh. He was sick all week."

"I know. How is he now?"

"Better. He wants to talk to you."

"Aunt Jessie?" Josh's high-pitched voice came on the line.

I was about to say hi when I heard Alex talking in the background. "You shouldn't call her Aunt Jessie," he was saying.

That surprised me. I didn't mind when Josh called me that.

"Why not?" Josh asked him.

"Because she's not your real aunt," I heard Alex explain. "It's confusing."

"But I'm not confused," Josh told him stubbornly.

"Alex is right, Josh," I said into the phone, trying not to let the hurt show in my voice. But inside I felt sick. I knew why Alex had brought this up. He felt the strain in our relationship. How could he not? It was his way of letting me know that everything wasn't all right with us, no matter how much we pretended it was. "So, how are you, sweetie?" I asked Josh, trying to sound light.

"I'm good. Uncle Alex is really sick, though."

"I know. Will you take good care of him for me?"

"Sure. I'll tell him more jokes." I heard Alex groan in the background. "I've been telling Uncle Alex jokes all day."

Josh was such a great kid. I would really miss him if . . . well, if Alex and I ever broke up. But I didn't want to think about that. Right now the prospect seemed too real, too awful. I'd had a taste of loneliness these last few days and I didn't like it—not at all—but I had nobody to blame but myself.

I just hoped I could make it all right somehow.

I raised my hand to knock on Kerri's apartment door, and hesitated. *Should I let things cool off before I talk to her?* I wondered. No. I had to settle things before it got worse.

The door suddenly opened, and I jumped back a little.

"Oh, Jessica," Liz said, a little startled too. "I was just leaving." She pointed to a youngish guy with a ponytail, trailing behind her. "You've met my boyfriend, Chuck, right?"

"Hi," I said to him, and he nodded.

"Erin's already here," Liz continued. "They're in Kerri's room. Go right in."

"Thanks, Liz," I said as she left with Chuck. Then I crossed through the living room to the hall that led to Kerri's bedroom. I stopped when I reached her doorway.

"Can you believe my mom is still going out with that guy?" Kerri was saying to Erin. Kerri was sitting on the mauve area rug in the center of her room. "I mean he's like, ten years younger than—" She stopped when she spotted me. "What are you doing here?"

"I—I just thought I'd stop by," I stammered. "Do you mind?"

Kerri shrugged. "Whatever."

I stepped into the room and sat next to Erin on Kerri's day bed. "Look, I just want to tell you again how sorry I—"

"Save it for someone who cares," Kerri cut in. "You totally dumped us, and then you come here, and expect—

"Stop it, you guys!" Erin cried. "There's something more important we need to talk about—Maya." She stared at me. "Luke so wants to go out with her, but she won't even talk to him. It's like she's afraid or something."

I shook my head. "Just because she's not into

Luke, that doesn't mean there's something seriously wrong with her."

"Oh, come on, Jessica," Kerri said. "Where have you been? Oh, yeah. We know where you've been. Sneaking around to college parties without us."

I bit my lip. "I said I was sorry."

"Okay, drop it," Erin said.

"I'm really sorry, Erin. I never meant to hurt you either."

She shrugged and looked away, making me wonder if I should even be there.

"Listen, Jess," Kerri said, "the whole Luke thing isn't the only stuff that's going on with Maya lately. We thought talking with her last Sunday had really helped. But she's still acting weird."

"What else is going on?" I felt really self-conscious having to ask Kerri to fill me in, but I tried to stop thinking about myself. I wanted to focus on Maya.

"For one thing, she never returns our calls or answers our e-mail, and she's been cutting classes left and right," Kerri said.

"And she hasn't shown up in the cafeteria for lunch all week," Erin added.

As I listened to the two of them discussing Maya, I realized how much closer they were to her than I was right now. Kerri, Erin, and Maya were still tight, hanging out together all day, every day, eating lunch, sharing classes, sending e-mails.

I wasn't a part of all that anymore, at least, not once I walked out of high school after third period. I'd been so wrapped up in my college life that I had forgotten about everything else.

God. I was even more horrible than I'd realized. Maya was in serious trouble, and I hadn't even noticed!

Chapter 16

"Jess, wait up!" Alex called to me on Monday morning.

I turned and saw him rushing down the hall, just as I was about to enter my homeroom. He looked pale and he had huge dark circles under his eyes.

"What are you doing here?" I asked him. "You look like you're still sick."

"I am, but I had to do some stuff for yearbook, so I couldn't stay home." He held up a hand as I leaned up to kiss him. "No, don't."

I was startled by his sharp tone. We always kissed each other hello. Did he know somehow, about Scott and me and Friday night? I wondered with a sense of dread. Kerri wouldn't have told him, just to get me back, would she?

"Germs," he said then, and I was relieved. But not for long.

There was an impatient look in his eyes—as if he

had something he wanted to discuss. I got a sinking feeling.

"Listen, Jessica," he said, "I need to ask you something, but I don't want a whole big scene about it."

Oh, God. Here it comes, I thought. *He knows about Scott and me, and he's going to break up with me right here in the hall.*

"Do you have the outlines for those feature articles?"

"For yearbook?" I went slack with relief. I couldn't believe it. "No, I didn't have time to do them over the weekend," I said. "But I promise I will as soon as—"

Alex cut me off. "I needed them first thing this morning."

I looked at him in surprise. His tone was so cold, and the way he'd interrupted me—well, it wasn't like him.

"I'm sorry, Alex," I said. "But I had to do this paper all day yesterday, and—"

"Forget it," he said. "I don't have time for excuses."

"They're not excuses. Schoolwork has to come before extracurricular stuff, Alex. You know that."

"You're right," he said. "And I'm sorry. I didn't mean to snap at you."

"It's okay," I told him. "I just have a lot going on right now. But I'll work on the outlines after class this afternoon," I reassured him. "And I'll e-mail them to you. It shouldn't take long."

Alex shook his head. "That won't work, Jessica. I needed them today—*this morning*." He glanced around the hallway, then back at me. "I have to find a new features editor."

"What?" I gaped at him. "You're *firing* me? You can't be serious."

"I'm sorry," he said quietly. "It's just that I can't pick up your slack anymore. I've been busy too, and I haven't been able to rely on you lately. I don't think you have enough time to do this job."

I couldn't believe he was actually firing me! I'd worked too hard to get this position. I couldn't let him just kick me off, just like that.

"Listen, Alex. I know you're upset. But I'm not giving up my job as features editor. I'll get the outlines to you by lunch. And I'll find the time to put in more work on the yearbook. I promise."

Alex's mouth twisted into a frown. "Sorry, Jess. I've made up my mind. Believe me, it wasn't easy. But I just can't cover for you anymore."

"This isn't fair," I told Alex. "You could have given me another chance to prove myself. You're supposed to be my boyfriend!"

Alex opened his mouth to speak, but then the bell rang. Kids began to hurry through the halls.

I turned and went into my class without saying another word to him.

All day I thought about how angry I was with Alex for firing me. I was still pondering it when I got home after class at the university. Okay, maybe he was right about me slacking off, but he could have given me a warning or something instead of just canning me.

The phone rang, shaking me from my thoughts. *Maybe it's Alex,* I thought as I answered it.

"Hey, Jess. How's it goin'?"

My stomach dropped when I figured out who it was. Scott.

I was so stunned at first that I didn't know what to say. Then I let him have it. "I can't believe you have the nerve to call me after what you did!"

"What did I do?"

"You were with Bree!"

"You found out," he said quietly. "I'm sorry. I was really wasted, and after the way you rejected me—"

"Rejected you?" I repeated.

"Yeah, when you shoved me away like you did. That really bummed me out."

"I said that I wasn't ready to go any further. And

you said that it was okay."

"Yeah, it is okay," he said. "But I'm not used to having a relationship without sex."

"Is that what this is?" I asked. He'd caught me off guard. "Is this a relationship?"

"If you want it to be," he whispered.

"Do you?" I asked, not exactly sure what to make of all this.

"Yeah," he said. "I do."

What was I supposed to say to that? I closed my eyes for a second and remembered how Scott's kisses made me feel. But then I thought about the night of the party. How he'd acted when I'd said no. How as soon as I left, he jumped in bed with Bree.

"How do I know I can trust you?" I asked at last. "You fooled around with my friend behind my back."

"First of all, nothing happened with Bree."

"I saw you two in that room, on the bed!"

"Yeah, but we just kissed, and then she passed out."

I thought about that. I didn't know whether to believe him. Bree had been pretty drunk that night. And she hadn't been in sociology class this afternoon, so I didn't have a chance to confront her. His word was all I had to go on.

I should probably just forget about Scott, and move on, I knew. But now that he was explaining his side of the story, it wasn't that simple.

"Besides," Scott went on, "You're the one who has the boyfriend, remember? You're not exclusively seeing me, either."

"True," I said. He had a point there.

"So what do you want to do?" Scott asked me.

"I'm not sure," I told him. That was the trouble. I wasn't sure about anything. And even though I was angry with Alex, I knew all this wasn't fair to him. Alex was a fantastic guy. He was more than just my boyfriend—more than a friend. I loved him.

That's why I had to break up with him as soon as possible.

Chapter 17

It felt really weird walking through the halls of South Central on Tuesday morning. All around me were crowds of kids, talking and joking with each other as they headed to their homerooms.

But even though I was in the midst of all these people, I felt totally alone.

I usually ran into Alex first thing in the morning too. So far today, I hadn't seen him. It wasn't that I planned to break up with him right here, right now . . . but I did want to tell him we had to talk. I didn't want to lose my nerve.

Kerri, Erin, and Maya hadn't met me at our usual spot by the cement steps at the front entrance of the school this morning. I guessed they hadn't forgiven me. I guessed I deserved it.

Then I spotted Erin and Kerri, standing in front of Kerri's locker, which was right across from mine. They were both looking at the latest issue of

seventeen magazine.

I tried not to look at them as I opened my locker and pulled out a book. But then I noticed that Erin was trying to catch my eye. She smiled a little, making me wonder if I should go over there.

I did.

"What's up?" I asked them.

Kerri just gave me a dirty look and went back to the magazine.

"I wanted to tell you something," Erin said. "We went to the mall last night to pick up my homecoming dress, and then we decided to drop by Maya's on the way home. Her father wasn't home, so she asked us to stay and hang out."

"You did?" I asked, a little hurt that they hadn't called me to come over too. I mean, I could understand why they didn't want me shopping with them, but Kerri and Erin knew that I wanted to be there for Maya at least.

Erin nodded. "And when the whole T.J. thing came up she said that she's going to talk to Kerri's mom about maybe finding some professional help. She admitted that she might need to talk to someone about it. Someone other than her friends."

"Are you serious?" I asked.

"No, we're lying," Kerri said sarcastically. Then she sighed. "Maya didn't want to at first, but then she seemed kind of relieved when we bugged her about it, and she finally said she would. So don't worry about Maya anymore. We took care of it."

"That's great," I said. I just stared at them. Things were so different all of a sudden. I found myself trying to think of something else to say to them, but I couldn't. I was starting to wonder how well I really knew any of my friends—and how well they knew me.

Kerri ignored me and flipped a page of the magazine. "I still think you should have bought this one, Erin," she said, pointing to a strappy pale pink dress with black embroidery. "It really says homecoming queen."

"No way." Erin shook her head. "I told you. I'm going totally vintage for this."

They had no idea that I was planning to break things off with Alex, and I couldn't bring myself to tell them. A few weeks ago, I would never have kept anything like this from them. Now . . . well, maybe I was afraid they'd take sides in the breakup—and wouldn't choose mine.

Kerri sighed and shoved the magazine into her backpack. She looked at Erin. "Well, I've got to get to homeroom."

"Me too." Erin glanced at me. "Um, see you in chorus, I guess."

I just stood there, watching my best friends disappear in the crowd.

On Wednesday afternoon, Bree showed up late for sociology.

"Hey, Jess," she said as she slid into her seat right before class started. I wondered if she was late because she hadn't wanted to talk to me. She usually showed up kind of early, like I did. She dropped my flowered duffel bag next to my chair. "Here's your stuff."

"Thanks," I said, keeping my gaze focused on my notes. I knew I had to say something to her about what had happened, but I couldn't figure out how to do it. She was acting as though nothing had happened.

"So did you have a good time at the party with Scott?"

That caught me off guard. I turned and looked at her. She was totally nonchalant, which made me angry.

Before I could say anything else, the professor called for quiet. Then the lecture was underway, and there was nothing I could do but steam. I couldn't believe it was so easy for Bree to pretend we were all buddy-buddy when she had been all over Scott the minute my back was turned.

As soon as class was over, she leaped out of her seat. "I've got to run," she called to me over her shoulder. "I'm meeting my lab partner in two minutes across campus, and I'm late."

I watched her disappear. Obviously she wasn't going to say anything to me about what had happened between her and Scott—and obviously she didn't know I knew.

I couldn't believe that I had ever thought Bree was my friend. But I didn't care about her, and I wasn't going to waste my time getting into a fight with her over Scott. It wasn't worth it.

I had other things to worry about. Like Alex. He'd been out sick Tuesday and today. I still hadn't had the chance to talk to him.

Friday morning was the beginning of homecoming weekend, and Alex still wasn't in school. After homeroom, I went to the pay phone and called his house. His mother answered the phone.

"Hi, Mrs. McKay. Is Alex okay?"

"Actually, I'm taking him to the doctor now."

"Can I please talk to him? Only for a second," I added.

"Sure," she said. Was it my imagination, or did she hesitate a little before she said it? Did she know things weren't right between us? It didn't seem likely that Alex would confide in his mother, but I could have sworn she seemed a little stiff when she said, "Hang on a second, and I'll go get him."

It took him a long time to pick up the phone. I stood there in the jammed hallway, trying to hear what they were saying to each other.

Were he and his mother holding a whispered conversation? Was he telling her he didn't want to talk to me, and asking her to make up some excuse? I couldn't hear a thing, other than the slamming locker doors and students' voices in the hallway.

Finally Alex picked up. "Hello?"

As soon as I heard his voice, I felt like crying. He sounded awful. "You're so sick," I said. "Oh, Alex, I feel so bad."

"Why? It's just a cold," he croaked. "But my mother's making me go to the doctor."

"Yeah, she told me." I cleared my throat. There was nothing left to say. "Good luck."

"Yeah, thanks. You too. Good luck tonight at homecoming. Sorry I can't be your escort."

"That's okay," I said. "I guess I'll make Ricky stand on the float with me." Going without Alex was going to feel so weird—like it was the beginning of doing lots of things on my own.

"Still, I'm sorry," he repeated. "I definitely would have been there for you if I wasn't sick."

All the anger I felt toward him for firing me disappeared. He really cared about me, even after the way I'd treated him lately. I didn't know what to say next.

"I have to go," he said.

"Me too," I told him. "Bye."

I hung up the phone, wiping at the tears that kept spilling out, and hoping nobody was looking.

Chapter 18

"It gives me great pleasure to announce this year's South Central High homecoming queen," Ms. Tominski, the vice principal, said into a microphone that evening at homecoming.

The sound system let out a high-pitched squeak. I glanced at Erin, who was beside me, looking beautiful in an ice blue 1920s flapper dress with fringe, and an amazing beaded headdress. "I hope you win," I mouthed to her.

We were standing on a platform in the middle of the football field. My brother Ricky fiddled with his tie as all the candidates and their escorts waited for the queen to be announced. A huge mass of cheering students and visiting alumni surrounded us in the crowded stands.

Erin gazed at me for a second, then grabbed my hand. "I hope you win, Jessica," she whispered, touching the shoulder of my simple black velvet sheath. "You look so sophisticated with your hair in a French twist." She smiled. "It's so ooh-la-la!"

I smiled back at her. I was so grateful to hear those words—not that I deserved to win; I had handed in my essay at the last minute—but because I knew Erin was willing to forgive me. I'd have to earn her trust again, I knew, but at least she was going to give me the chance to do that.

Kerri was another story. She still wouldn't even look at me.

Ms. Tominski cleared her throat again. "And the winner is . . ."

Erin and I both held our breath waiting for the answer.

"Erin Yamada!"

"You won, Erin!" I cried, thrilled.

Erin threw her arms around me, then turned to Glen, and gave him a huge kiss.

I caught the expression on his face. He was definitely in love with her.

And who could help it? She was adorable and bubbly and smiling as she and Glen posed for pictures alone and with the rest of us.

The cameras continued to flash as we made our way to the convertibles parked on the track. The band played "Onward, Lions," our school song, which was set to the tune of "On, Wisconsin," as we were driven around the field a few times.

I could see my parents in the crowd, clapping wildly as I rode by. It was good to know I'd done something to make them so proud, even though I hadn't won. My grandmother was with them, and she caught my eye and gave me two thumbs-up. I was glad she was there.

"This is fun, huh, Jess?" Ricky asked.

I nodded. It really was fun, to my surprise.

Everything would have been perfect, except . . .

I kept thinking about Alex.

He should have been here with me. He should have been enjoying this too. It was the kind of thing he lived for—all this school spirit, and everything. We were seniors. There wouldn't be another chance for this, and he was missing it.

There wouldn't be another chance for us, either. After tomorrow—or whenever I managed to work up my nerve to tell him—we wouldn't be together anymore.

I felt sick when I thought of that.

"What's wrong?" Ricky asked as we circled the field.

"Nothing." I put a smile on my face and waved to the crowd like I was supposed to.

The car Ricky and I were sitting in slowed, pulling toward the parking space near the entrance to the locker room. I kept waving as we all piled out onto the field again.

I spotted Maya in the bleachers. At first I thought she was sitting by herself—Kerri was down in front, with the cheerleaders.

Then I noticed that Luke Perez was in the row behind Maya. As I watched, he leaned over and said something to her. She shook her head and said something back to him, then started to stand up.

Luke reached out to touch her arm, and Maya jumped back, losing her balance. I gasped when she almost fell off the bleachers. Luke tried to help her, but Maya just took off.

I wanted to go after her, but I hesitated. After all that had happened lately, maybe she wouldn't want me to. I was sure Kerri told her that I'd lied about the party. Maybe she didn't feel close to me either. Then I realized that we had been friends for too many years. Our relationship wasn't going to fade or die. We were just going through a rough patch. I had to be there for her if she needed me.

"I've got to go do something," I told Ricky. I turned and raced after Maya.

It wasn't easy to run in my long, fitted dress. But I hiked it up and stumbled along. I caught up with Maya just as she reached the foot of the bleachers. Luke was right behind her.

"Maya!" I said. "What's wrong?"

She didn't say anything, just kept going.

"What did you say to her?" I asked Luke, who looked confused.

"Nothing!" he protested. "I just asked her if she wanted to go out sometime. What's up with her? Is she okay?"

"I don't know," I called back to him as I took off after Maya. I caught up with her by the entrance gate.

"Maya!" I shouted, and this time, she turned around. I saw that her face was tear-stained. I ran to her and put my arm around her. "What's wrong?"

"Nothing," she said in a shaky voice.

"You can talk to me, Maya," I said. "Please. I know I haven't been around much lately, but I'm here for you. Really. I want to help."

"I don't need your help," she said. "I just want to go home. Okay?"

I stared at her, feeling awful. Would she have felt this way a few weeks ago?

Maya wouldn't meet my eyes.

"Okay," I said quietly, and let her leave.

As everyone headed over to the homecoming dance in the gym, I went out to the parking lot, to find my mom's car. Part of me wanted to stick around because it was the last homecoming dance I'd ever go to. But without Alex there, I knew it wouldn't be much fun.

When I got home I would send him a quick e-mail, just to tell him how the homecoming ceremony went and all. But after that, I knew, Alex and I had some serious talking to do.

I was so wrapped up in my thoughts about Alex, I didn't even notice Scott's car, parked right next to mine, until I was only a few feet away. Scott sat in his car, listening to a Smash Mouth tape. A huge smile crossed his face when he spotted me.

"Wow. You look hot," he said.

"What are you doing here?" I asked him.

"I called you this afternoon," he explained. "Your dad said you were out with your mom shopping for a homecoming dress. Why didn't you tell me you were running for homecoming?"

"You still didn't answer my question," I told him, rubbing my bare arms against the cold. I really wanted to get into my mom's car.

"I just wanted to see you," he said. "I guess I felt bad the way it ended up on the phone the other day. I wanted to talk to you some more."

"Oh. Okay," I said. I felt really surprised. I didn't think he really cared that much about me, but maybe I'd been wrong.

"So, how'd it go?" he asked. "Did you win?"

"No. My friend Erin did."

"Are you upset?"

"I'm okay," I said.

"I bet you're probably glad it's over." He leaned over and opened the door on the passenger side for me. "Come on, get in. Just to talk. You look like you're freezing out there."

I was freezing. And I guessed it would be good to talk things out with him in private. Shivering, I stepped into the car.

Scott started the car and turned the heat on.

"Thanks." I slipped my feet out of my shoes and wiggled my toes. I thought about telling him about Maya, but then I realized he probably wouldn't really care about that.

"Listen, Jess. I think you got it wrong about me." He turned toward me and put his hand on my shoulders. "I really like you. I respect you. Sex isn't all I think about. . . ."

"I know," I said defensively.

"Although . . . when I'm around you, I do think about it quite a bit," he added, leaning closer.

He kissed me deeply, and my body responded automatically. I wrapped my arms around his neck so that we were pressed closer. We kissed some more. Then I felt his hand moving on my breasts.

I tensed up.

"What is it?" he asked, stopping. "What's wrong?"

What was wrong? Everything was wrong. He'd said he wanted to talk. This wasn't exactly talking.

"I just . . ." I forced myself to stop touching him, to pull backward. I looked up into his gorgeous face. "You said you just wanted to talk," I reminded him.

"I do," he said. He paused and looked off over my shoulder, as if he was trying to figure out what he wanted to tell me. "I keep thinking you're so sophisticated and all, because you come across that way. It's hard to remember that you're still inexperienced about a lot of things, and I can't forget that. I would never want to hurt you."

"You haven't."

"No, but I could. This thing that's going on between us just sort of came out of nowhere, and I don't know what's going to happen. I mean, I want to go back to New York, and you have to finish high school . . ."

"What are you saying, Scott?"

"I'm saying I still want to see you, if you want to see me. But it's not a bad idea to slow things down. Let's just take it easy. Just hang out a bit. Not get too involved."

Not get too involved? I said to myself. *He didn't*

feel that way when he thought I was going to have sex with him!

I was outraged, and a little embarrassed. But at the same time I kind of felt relieved. This thing with Scott would never work. He didn't really care about me. And even though he was sexy, there had to be more than that to a relationship.

"You're right," I told him. And suddenly, all I wanted to do was go home.

He looked at me. "You all right?"

"I'm fine. I've just got to get going, that's all."

"Okay, if you say so." He gave me a light, gentle kiss on the cheek. "I'll call you. I really will."

"Sure." I opened the car door, and stepped out into the parking lot, thinking about how crazy some girls might think I was for walking away from a guy like Scott. But I didn't care.

I leaned on the door and gazed into Scott's eyes. "You know what?" I told him. "Don't bother."

Chapter 19

When I woke up the next morning, I checked my e-mail. I don't know what I was hoping to find. Maybe something from Alex about wanting to get together. Then we'd finally get to talk.

There was nothing from him. But I did have a message from Maya.

> **Jessica, give me a call on my cell phone when you read this.**
> **Maya**

It was dated last night. I signed off so I could phone her. But after I got dressed and went downstairs, I found Ricky on the kitchen phone.

"I need to make a call," I told him.

"You don't own the phone," he replied. "I'll be off soon."

Grabbing a magazine, I sat in the living room to

wait. After twenty minutes I could hear he was still talking. "Ricky!" I yelled, returning to the kitchen. "I want the phone."

He turned his back to me and kept talking. With a deep, angry huff of breath, I went to the closet and yanked my jacket out. Maybe I'd just go over there.

On my way to Maya's, I passed by Alex's house. His sister-in-law, Betsy, was walking down the driveway toward her car, which was parked at the curb. I gave a honk, and she waved to me.

I pulled up alongside her car. "Coming to see Alex?" she asked with a friendly smile.

"Not really, but . . . how's he feeling?"

"A lot better," she told me. "He'd probably like some company. Why don't you go in?"

"Oh." I hesitated, wondering if I should stay. "Is anyone else home?"

"Dave took Josh to miniature golf, and Mom and Dad had tickets to the Packers game."

"Oh," I murmured again.

"I've got to get to work," Betsy said, climbing into her car. "The door's open."

I guessed this was the chance I'd been waiting so long for. Alex was feeling better, and he was alone. I pulled into the driveway, parked, and let myself in the front door.

I stood there in the hallway, listening to the quiet

house, inhaling its familiar scent of home cooking and lemon furniture polish. I looked around at the framed photos on the walls—most of them of Alex and Dave through the years, and some more recent ones, too—Dave and Betsy at their wedding, and several of Josh.

I had always assumed that someday, there would be a picture of Alex and me on our wedding day, and pictures of our children too. I had pretty much considered myself a part of the family, and until the past few weeks, it hadn't really occurred to me that I might not join the family officially. Now it hit me that this might be the last time I would be in this house. I'd miss his family. I'd miss Josh most of all.

What about Alex? a tiny voice in my head asked.

Oh, God. I hadn't wanted to allow myself to think about how much I'd miss Alex. He had been a part of my life every day for two years. It was impossible to imagine cutting him out, just like that.

What would we do when we saw each other in school? How would we act when we passed in the halls, or when we found ourselves at the same parties? Who would take me to the senior prom?

Even more upsetting . . . who would Alex take?

Imagining him with another girl—dancing with her, smiling at her, kissing her—was so painful it nearly snatched my breath away. I couldn't stand the thought of someone else with my boyfriend.

I was the one who belonged in Alex's arms. *Then why did you cheat on him with Scott?* I asked myself. But I couldn't change what I had done. And I couldn't have it both ways.

If I wasn't prepared to give one hundred percent of myself to Alex, then I needed to give him up—no matter how much I still loved him. And I did love him. I really did.

I wiped a tear from my eye and started slowly up the stairs, dragging my hand along the old wooden banister. At the top of the flight, I paused in the hallway, staring at his closed door.

I wanted to run down the stairs and out the door and just keep running. But I couldn't. I'd been running long enough, and I realized that in the end, there was no escape.

I knocked softly on Alex's door, telling myself that if he didn't answer, I wouldn't go in. I couldn't wake him from a sound sleep. I'd just have to wait until another time to—

"Betsy?" he called.

"No," I said, turning the knob and opening the door. "It's me."

"Jessica," he said, surprised. "I just sent you an e-mail." He was in bed, leaning against a pile of pillows. There was a lot of stuff spread out all over the bed around him, and it took me a minute to realize what it was.

"About what?"

"I wanted to know if you ever finished that list of quotes we were going to use on the first seniors' page," he asked. "I mean, before I let you go."

"You're working on the yearbook now, while you're sick?" I asked, sitting carefully at the foot of the bed so I wouldn't mess up the pictures and sheets of text he'd carefully arranged.

"Yeah. This layout is due Monday morning, and I really wanted to do it myself," he said, fiddling with the ruler in his hand.

I picked up a glossy black-and-white picture and looked at it. It was one of Alex and me, arm in arm, sitting on the bleachers in the sunshine. My head was tilted up toward his face, and his mouth was open, like he was telling me something. It must have been something funny, because I had this huge grin on my face. Neither of us seemed to have noticed the camera.

"I never knew anyone took this picture," I said.

"It was a candid shot," he told me. "I'm not sure if I'm going to use it yet."

I noticed that Alex was wearing the polo shirt I'd brought back for him from my family's summer vacation up in Minnesota, and I realized, with a start, that this hadn't been snapped last spring after all. It must have been taken just a few weeks ago, after school had started again.

Had we really been that happy so recently? How had everything changed so fast?

I took a deep breath. "We need to talk," I said.

To my shock, he nodded. "I know."

"You do?"

"Yeah." He shrugged. "It's pretty obvious, Jess."

"What is?" Did he know about Scott? Had someone told him?

"Just that things have been kind of weird between us for a while. What's up with you?"

So he didn't know about Scott. I was relieved.

Being honest didn't mean spilling the whole sordid story. It didn't mean that I had to tell him what I had done. It would hurt him too much. I just had to let him know how I felt.

"Alex, I think we need more space," I said, my voice shaking slightly. I turned and forced myself to look him in the eye. "I want us to keep seeing each other, but I think we should give each other room to breathe. . . ."

He didn't say anything. I couldn't tell, from his expression, what he was thinking. He was just looking at me, staring at me like he was waiting for me to continue.

So I took a deep breath and spilled the final part. The hard part. "And I think we need to let each other see other people."

He didn't say anything. I couldn't take the silence. I looked down at my hands.

"You're right, Jess."

Stunned, I looked up to see him nodding. I hadn't expected him to agree. I had thought he would protest, that he would be angry, that he would fight for me or something. Now, finding out that he felt the same way, I felt really . . . hurt.

"We're only seventeen, Jessica," he said. "After seeing what my brother and Betsy have gone through—and they're only a little older than us— well, you know that's not what I want. Maybe you're right. Maybe our relationship was getting a little too heavy."

Now that I knew he wasn't going to talk me into going back to the way things were, I had to face the fact that things really had changed for good. We really weren't going to be a couple anymore—not the way we had been.

"I still love you," I burst out.

"I still love you too," he said, opening his arms.

I threw myself into them, burying my head against his shoulder. It was so comforting to have him hold me that I never wanted to let go.

But I did. I leaned back, and I gazed at him. "This is so hard," I said, sobbing. "But we can still go out sometimes, right?"

He shook his head. "No. I don't think so."

"What do you mean?" I cried. "You just said you still love me!"

"I do," he answered.

"But this makes no sense," I argued, as tears began to stream down my cheeks.

"It makes total sense," he insisted. "Maybe our relationship was too intense, but I can't just be some guy you date once in a while. I'm sorry, Jess, but it doesn't work that way." He looked away from me, and I could tell that he was crying. "It would be too hard—for both of us."

"I guess that's it, then," I said, a little frightened at the prospect of facing the world without Alex. A part of me didn't even want to leave the comfort of his room. But I had to. Alex had been my first love, and now it was over.

I wasn't sure what my life would be like once I stepped out that door. All I knew was, I couldn't look back.

I drove home feeling strangely calm. Alex wasn't in my life anymore. It seemed impossible, and yet it was true.

Scott was gone too, but somehow that didn't really affect me. It almost seemed as if I'd dreamed him—that he'd never actually been part of my life at all.

But then a knot of worry tightened in my stomach as I thought of Maya. I needed to call her as soon as I got home.

Maybe she was finally ready to talk about what had happened at homecoming. I knew how much confiding in a friend could help.

As I pulled into my driveway, I saw Kerri standing on the porch with my mother. Her arms were folded across her chest. Her brows furrowed as she watched me park.

She probably came over here to yell at me, I thought, sighing. I wasn't willing to get into another fight with Kerri. I couldn't—not so soon after breaking up with Alex. I was exhausted.

Kerri ran up to the car as I climbed out, a scowl on her face.

"Kerri, look, I know you hate me, but I can't fight with you right now, okay?"

To my surprise, Kerri wrapped her arms around me and hugged me tightly. She started crying. "Forget about that, Jess. It's over, okay?" She pulled away from me, desperately searching my eyes. "Please tell me you were with Maya."

I shook my head slowly. "I haven't seen her since the homecoming game. She said she was going home. She e-mailed me last night."

"Probably from her palm pilot." Kerri stared at me intensely. "She never came home last night, Jess," she said. "Maya's missing!"

Here's a sneak peek at

TURNING
seventeen #3

For Real
Maya's Story

"Where have you been? We've been so worried!" Kerri dragged me into the kitchen of her apartment. Erin and Jessica jumped to their feet when they saw me.

"Maya! Are you all right?" Jessica cried.

"Where were you?" Erin demanded.

"I'm sorry," I said, feeling sheepish. "I was just driving around."

"All night?" Jessica asked.

"Well, I parked at the university. I slept in my car."

They stared at me in shock. "You slept in your car?" Erin repeated.

"I—I just couldn't go home," I admitted.

"Maya, your dad came to my house this morning, looking for you," Jessica said. "He's really upset."

Kerri picked up the phone. "You've got to call him," she insisted.

"I know," I said, biting my lip. "I'm just not ready yet. What am I going to say to him? He's going to kill me!"

"Maya!" Kerri's hand still gripped the cordless. "You have to call."

"Look, Ker, don't make me call him just yet," I pleaded. "I've got to decide what to tell him."

Kerri sighed. "Fine. You want some breakfast first? Will that give you some courage?"

"I hope so," I replied. Jessica, Erin, and I sat down at the table while Kerri made her famous waffles.

"We're really worried about you, Maya," Erin said.

"You can't go on like this," Jessica added. "Missing school, staying in bed all day, not caring about anything. And we—" She paused and looked at Kerri and Erin. "We don't know how to help you. This whole thing has kind of spiraled out of control."

"I know," I whispered.

"Spending the day in bed is one thing," Kerri put in. "But spending the night in a parking lot?" She dropped into the chair next to me. "Maybe you should talk to someone. You know, my mom could give you a referral to a therapist if you want."

Liz Hopkins, Kerri's mom, was a guidance counselor at a junior high. I knew she meant well. But the idea of telling a total stranger all of my problems made my stomach hurt.

I shook my head, blinking back tears. "I'm not

going to a shrink. And I don't think my dad would like it."

"Maya, your dad already knows something is seriously wrong," Jessica said. "You didn't go home last night."

Kerri set a plate of waffles in front of me. I stared at it, suddenly not hungry anymore.

Maybe if I did have someone to talk to, I thought, *someone I could open up to who would be impartial, who didn't know any of the people at South Central . . . maybe that would make me feel a little less confused.*

"Maya! I'm so glad you're all right." Liz Hopkins walked into the room, dressed in a mauve bodysuit and gray leggings. She came over to me and squeezed my shoulder. "You gave us all a scare." She glanced at the phone. "Please tell me you've called your dad to let him know you're safe."

I shrugged, embarrassed. "No, not yet."

Liz shook her head, her lips pinched together. "You have to call your father. Or let me, if it's easier."

"Could you call?" Then I hesitated. "Um, Liz, I was thinking. . . ." I took a breath and summoned all my courage. "Could you, um, that is, would you be willing to give me the name of someone who maybe I could talk to?"

"Say no more." Liz picked up a writing tablet and

scribbled down a name. "Valerie Sheridan. She's very good and very nice. You'll like her."

I took the piece of paper she handed me, and started for the door. "Please tell my dad I'm on my way home."

The automatic sprinklers were coming on as I unlocked our massive front door and tiptoed into the foyer. My friends and I called the big, cold, empty house where I lived "the castle." As usual, everything looked immaculate and smelled of lemons. The castle is a decorator's dream, but not exactly cozy. I missed our old small, suburban house in Kensington Heights, where I grew up with Erin, Jessica, and Kerri. When I told Erin we were moving to a mini-mansion near Lake Monona, she shrieked with glee. "You're so lucky!" she cried. "Those houses are gorgeous!"

I didn't feel lucky. I didn't like the cold marble floors or the spotless white living room out of *Architectural Digest*. And Dad and I didn't really need four bathrooms.

My dad rushed toward me from the living room and gave me a quick, hard hug.

"Maya! Are you all right?"

I nodded. "I'm fine. Really."

"Where on earth were you all night? I was worried sick."

"I—I was just driving around," I stammered. "I felt kind of confused . . . and I fell asleep in the car."

I saw relief in his blue eyes, then a flash of anger. "Into my study. Now."

Silently I followed him, cringing as my eyes met Betty's. Betty was our housekeeper. She made sure my dad and I had a well-balanced diet, and she kept our house neat as a pin.

Once inside the study, Dad sat down at his desk and leaned back, his forehead creased. "Maya, I'm confused. You've always been so levelheaded. What got into you?" He shook his head. "Why would you do something like that?"

My mouth felt dry. I wished I could tell him about T.J. and how horrible I felt. But I couldn't. "I don't know, Dad," I mumbled. "I guess I've just been having a hard time lately."

"What you did is very serious, Maya. I'm afraid I'll have to ground you for a while."

I wasn't thrilled about being grounded. But then I thought, what difference did it make? There was nowhere I really wanted to go, anyway.

And at least I know he cares about me, I thought. *I guess that's better than nothing.*

Then he cleared his throat. "Enough about that. I need to talk to you, Maya. You know I'm going to be running for lieutenant governor."

I nodded. My dad had been meeting with political consultants for weeks. Our house was like a zoo sometimes, filled with advisers and lawyers and other bores in khakis and button-down shirts.

"Next week I'll officially toss my hat into the ring," Dad told me. "I'll be making a formal announcement."

"Wow, Dad. That's terrific," I said, not sure how I really felt. Life in the castle would be even more of a pressure cooker, I realized.

"It's going to be a rough campaign," my father went on. "I'll need to be able to rely on you, Maya. No more stunts like last night. The press is going to be watching me—and you—very closely."

"I'm sorry," I said truthfully. I slipped my hand into my pocket and felt the piece of paper Kerri's mother had given me. The paper with the therapist's name and number.

I took a deep breath. "I won't ever do that again, Dad, I promise," I said. "But Dad—I need help. I need someone to talk to. To help me deal with stuff."

"If you're having problems, Maya, you can come to me anytime."

"I know, but—" This was hard for me to say. "I think I need more than that. Liz Hopkins gave me the name of a therapist. She's supposed to be very good."

"A therapist?" my dad echoed.

I showed him the paper with Dr. Sheridan's name on it.

My dad studied the paper, frowning. He didn't say anything for a long time.

"Dad?" I asked. "What do you think? Can I call her?"

Dad crumpled the paper and tossed it into the trash can. "No," he said. "Absolutely not."

Don't miss the chance to
win a trip to New York City and hang out with
the editors of your favorite magazine!

GRAND PRIZE

- 3-day, 2-night trip to New York City
- Meeting with the editors of **seventeen**
- Fabulous makeover at a New York City salon

3 FIRST PRIZES

- Personal astrological readings

50 SECOND PRIZES

- Cool makeup bags filled with makeup

ENTER TO WIN

Fill out and mail to: HarperCollins Seventeen Sweepstakes
P.O. Box 8188
Grand Rapids, MN 55745-8188

_____

Name

_____

Date of Birth

_____

Parent/Legal Guardian (required if under 18)

_____

Address

_____

Address

_____

Phone

**One entry per person. No purchase necessary.
You must be between the ages of 13 and 21 to enter.
See back for official rules.**

Seventeen Sweepstakes Official Rules

NO PURCHASE NECESSARY. SWEEPSTAKES OPEN ONLY TO LEGAL U.S. RESIDENTS BETWEEN THE AGES OF 13 AND 21 YEARS AS OF 9/1/00. Employees (and their immediate families and those living in their same households) and all officers, directors, representatives, and agents of HarperCollins Publishers, Parachute Properties, **seventeen** magazine, and any of their affiliates, parents, subsidiaries, advertising and promotion and fulfillment agencies are not eligible. Sweepstakes starts 9/1/00, and ends on 1/1/01. By participating, entrants agree to these official rules.

To Enter: Entries will be used by HarperCollins only for purposes of this Sweepstakes. Hand print your name, complete street address, city, state, zip, and phone number on this official entry form or on a 3 x 5 card and send to: HarperCollins Seventeen Sweepstakes, PO Box 8188, Grand Rapids, MN 55745-8188. Limit one entry per person/family/household. One entrant per entry. HarperCollins Publishers is not responsible for lost, miscommunicated, late, damaged, incomplete, stolen, misdirected, illegible, or postage-due mail entries. Entry materials/data that have been tampered with, altered, or that do not comply with these rules are void. Entries become the property of HarperCollins Publishers Inc., and will not be returned or acknowledged. Entries must be postmarked by 1/1/01, and received no later than 1/8/01.

Drawing: Winners will be selected in a random drawing held on or about 1/9/01 by HarperCollins Publishers, whose decisions are final, from all eligible entries received. Winners will be notified by mail on or about 1/15/01. The prizes will be awarded in the name of minor's parent or legal guardian. Odds of winning depend on total number of eligible entries received.

Prizes: Grand Prize: One (1) Grand Prize Winner will receive a trip to New York City for two (2) people (winner and parent or legal guardian) for 3 days, 2 nights at a date to be determined in Spring 2001. Prize consists of round-trip coach class air transportation to and from winner's nearest served airport (U.S. citizens residing in the U.S. at the time of the trip), standard hotel accommodations for one room, two nights, a day with the editors of **seventeen** magazine, and a makeover at a New York City salon to be chosen by sponsor. Total approximate retail value (ARV) is $3,000.00. Travel/accommodation restrictions may apply. All other expenses not specifically stated are the sole responsibility of the winner. Winner must travel with winner's parent/legal guardian if winner is a minor in his/her state of residence. Travel and use of accommodation are at risk of winner and parent/legal guardian and HarperCollins, Parachute, and **seventeen** magazine do not assume any liability. First-place prize: 3 First Place Prize winners will each receive a personal astrological reading by an astrologer chosen by sponsor, the time and place to be determined at sponsor's sole discretion. Approximate retail value (ARV) is $500.00 each. Second-place Prize: 50 Second Prize Winners will each receive a special makeup bag filled with makeup. Approximate retail value (ARV) is $10.00 each. Total value of all prizes is $5,000.00. In the event Grand Prize Winner is unable to travel/accept prize during time specified, Grand Prize Winner shall be considered to have irrevocably forfeited prize and an alternate Grand Prize Winner will be selected. If any prize is not available or cannot be fulfilled, HarperCollins, Parachute, and **seventeen** magazine reserve the right to substitute a prize of equal or greater value. Prizes are not redeemable for cash value by winners.

General Conditions: By taking part in this Sweepstakes entrants agree to be bound by these official rules and by all decisions of HarperCollins Publishers, Parachute Publishing, and **seventeen** magazine. Winners or their parents/legal guardians, if minor in his/her state of residence, are required to sign and return an Affidavit of Eligibility and Liability Release and where legal, a Publicity Release within ten (10) days of notification. Failure to return documents as specified, or if prize notification or prize is returned as nondeliverable, may result in prize forfeiture and selection of an alternate winner. Grand Prize Winner and his/her travel companion must sign and return a Liability/Publicity Release prior to issuance of travel documents. Sweepstakes is subject to all applicable federal, state, and local laws and regulations and is void in Puerto Rico and wherever else prohibited by law. By participating, winners (and winners' parents/legal guardians, if applicable) agree that HarperCollins Publishers, Parachute, **seventeen** magazine, and their affiliate companies, parents, subsidiaries, advertising and promotion agencies, and all of their respective officers, directors, employees, representatives, and agents will have no liability whatsoever, and will be held harmless by all winners (and winners' parents/legal guardians, if applicable) for any liability for any injuries, losses, or damages of any kind to person, including death, and property resulting in whole or in part, directly or indirectly, from the acceptance, possession, misuse, or use of the prize, or participation in this Sweepstakes. Except where legally prohibited, by accepting prize, winners (and winners' parents/legal guardians, as applicable) grant permission for HarperCollins Publishers, Parachute, **seventeen** magazine, and those acting under their authority to use his/her name, photograph, voice and/or likeness, for advertising and/or publicity purposes without additional compensation. Taxes on prizes are solely the responsibility of the winners. Prizes are not transferable and cannot be assigned.

Prize Winners' Names: For the names of the Winners (available after 1/15/01), send a self-addressed stamped envelope for receipt by 1/31/01 to HarperCollins Seventeen Sweepstakes, PO Box 8105, Grand Rapids, MN 55745-8105.

Sponsored by HarperCollins Publishers, New York, NY 10019-4703.